The Naked Truth

Maggie Aldrich

Maggie Aldrich
www.maggiealdrichwrites.com
maggie@maggiealdrichwrites.com

Book Layout © 2017 BookDesignTemplates.com
Cover Design by Alchemy Book Covers and Design

The Naked Truth/Maggie Aldrich. -- 1st Ed.

Forever my family.

ACKNOWLEDGMENTS

The author wishes to acknowledge the invaluable assistance of the following: My fabulous beta readers Teresa, Karen, Vickie, Collin and Sydney; the bilingual genius Nathalí; the magnificent Melissa Kreikemeier of 808 Editorial; the creative Keri Knutson of Alchemy Book Covers and Design; the wonderful ChickLitChatHQ Facebook group; and all of my loyal readers. Your comments and encouragement keep me writing!

• PROLOGUE •

The past two years of my life have been filled with more turmoil, upheaval, joy, and sadness than the first thirty years combined. I lost my parents, my job, and my trust fund, was kicked out of my house, and abandoned by my cat. But I also met the man of my dreams, brought down the men that tried to steal my father's legacy, and found out that I'm a lot stronger and more resourceful than I ever gave myself credit for. Losing it all sure puts everything in perspective. And on the day that I gazed into Michael's eyes and said, "I do," I knew without a doubt that everything was back on track—until that fateful note appeared, and my life was once again turned upside down.

• CHAPTER 1 •

September 2016

My eyes fluttered open and I saw Michael gazing down at me, a look of concern etched on his face, eyes wide in alarm. The sleeves of his tuxedo shirt were rolled up, showing his strong, tanned forearms as he gently stroked my face, whispering something I strained to hear.

Oh, my boyfriend. God, he's beautiful. Wait—my husband! *Husband?* I got married today, right? This was my wedding day! Then what was I doing flat on my back with him and his brother-in-law, Jack, staring down at me, looking panicked? I mean, flat on my back with Michael above me any other day of the week would be *just fine.* But Jack, or any other person in this scenario for that matter, was not welcome! Was I in the middle of some weird, twisted fantasy?

No! My fantasies about Michael do not involve a third party! Ew, ew, ew!

My eyes swept over the two of them and I began to slightly panic as Jack held down my arms, putting pressure on my wrists. Why was he doing that? Michael gathered my hair and pulled it up off my neck. I tried to say something, but while their movements were swift, my body felt sluggish and weak. My mouth struggled to form words, but no sound came out.

I finally squeaked out something unintelligible. "Oh yeah, there she is," I heard Jack say, winking at Michael and smiling. Michael looked relieved as he began pushing my dress up toward my knees, letting the cool ocean air swirl around my legs. Why was Michael pushing my dress up *in front of Jack?!* How about some privacy, please! This was not what I had imagined for my wedding night. Not at all! Where was our secluded ocean-front B&B? I shook my head and struggled to break free of Jack's grip when Fritz's face appeared so close to mine that I could feel his breath on my face.

"What the hell is going on, Emily?" he asked gruffly. "Flat on your back already? Couldn't wait a few hours?" He grinned slightly and began unbuttoning his shirt, removing his tie. Oh. My. God. *This was not happening!* Fritz was not stripping! Jack was not holding my arms down while Michael pulled up my dress. This was a bad dream. A very bad dream! *Wake up, Emily! Wake up!*

My leg shot out and connected with something solid and I heard a loud "Oof!", followed by groaning and someone falling back against my legs. I could no longer see Michael, and Jack quickly let go of my arms and backed up with his hands in the air, choking out, "Oh man, Michael, you gotta watch out for this one!"

Fritz looked down at me, smiling and shaking his head. "That's my girl," he said as he gently helped me sit up.

"What happened?" I asked, breathless, finally finding my voice. "What's going on?" My head pounded, and I looked around, stunned to see our wedding guests still present and crowding around us, staring at us with a mixture of concern, surprise, and pity. It wasn't my wedding *night* after all. We were still at the reception on the beach in La Jolla. Relief flowed through me, followed quickly by confusion as I tried to remember what had happened.

"You fainted," Fritz explained, wiping the sand off my back. "And then when your knight in shining armor came to your rescue and tried to cool you off by pulling up your dress, you nailed him in the jimmy," he chuckled, "and not in a good way."

Fritz and Jack were laughing with glee as I looked down to see my new husband crouched in the fetal position, hands cupping his boy parts, eyes glazed over.

"Oh, babe, I'm so sorry!" I reached down to help him but instantly felt dizzy. My head swayed and I stumbled to one side.

"Watch it now," Jack said, clearing his throat and getting serious. He quickly returned to doctor mode. "You may have bumped your head when you fell on this...uh...sand." He looked around, trying to determine whether I had really hit my head on anything. "Regardless, you should let me check you out." Jack was a pediatrician in San Diego and the family dispenser of medical advice. "What happened? Are you literally swooning over the thought of being married to this guy here," he asked, jerking his thumb at Michael, "or is something wrong?"

I carefully sat back up as Michael struggled to do the same, giving me a pained smile while he gingerly moved around. "I'm okay," he squeaked out in a high voice. "Might need some ice." He sounded like Mickey Mouse and I began to giggle in spite of myself.

"I'm not sure what happened, Jack." I looked at the state of my beautiful wedding dress twisted around my legs and covered in sand. "I was talking to Father McDermott, and then..." I desperately tried to remember what had happened. Why had I fainted? I hadn't eaten much that day, and I knew I had normal wedding jitters, but I'm not a fainter. I don't think I'd ever fainted before in my life.

I looked around, trying to jar my memory. Seagulls swooped overhead and the ocean waves crashed rhythmically. Guests began to converse with each other again, assuming everything was under control. My best friend, Lisa, weaved her way toward us carrying a bag of ice and a glass of water. A small piece of paper fluttered in the wind nearby, tumbling down the beach. And, suddenly, I remembered.

• CHAPTER 2 •

"MY DAD! THAT NOTE WAS FROM MY DAD!" I grabbed at Jack and yanked myself up to standing, pulling him back down to his knees in the process. Kicking off my sandals and grabbing my skirt, I ran toward the paper swirling in the breeze, perilously close to the water. The sand mashed under my feet, and I stumbled as I got closer, feeling water splash up to my knees. Just as the ocean began to pull it under, I reached my hand down and snatched the notecard, lifting it, dripping, out of the Pacific. Frantically shaking it off, my eyes searched the page for the words he had written. My dad was alive! And this was the proof.

But there was nothing. Absolutely nothing. The card was blank.

I turned it over and over, shaking my head in disbelief, the paper seeming to disintegrate with every touch. There had been words on that piece of paper. Words written by my dad. I know his handwriting. It was undeniably his! He was alive and he had been right here!

I felt a hand on my shoulder and turned around to see Fritz struggling to catch his breath. In the distance, Michael took the ice pack from Lisa, held it against his crotch and looked at me, puzzled and clearly still in pain.

"Just before Father McDermott left," I started, looking at Fritz, "he gave me this note. It was from my dad, Fritz, I swear it was!"

Fritz shook his head slowly, as if not comprehending. "Emily, honey, your dad is dead." He looked at me with sympathy, his Santa Clause face still red from exertion. "Man, I need to get in shape," he muttered. He wiped the sweat from his forehead before looking at what I held in my hands. "Someone's got to be playing a mean trick on you. Let me see that paper." I tried to give it to him, but it stuck to my hands like glue. "I don't see any writing on it. Are you sure that's even paper?"

"Yes! I swear to you it wasn't blank before! He'd written me a note telling me I looked beautiful and thanking me for being careful. Fritz," I said, the wet notecard falling apart in my hands, now a big, gooey mess, "I know what I saw. You've got to believe me! There were words on this piece of paper before it hit the water. Ask Father." I glanced around for Father McDermott in vain, my heart beating out of control. Where had he gone? I had to talk to him. He might have been the only person to speak to my dad.

"Let me see that. Come on, let's go sit down and get you a drink." Fritz peeled the paper pulp from my hands and guided me over to the head table as the sun began to set behind us. Lantern lights were strung around the perimeter of the reception area and small candles twinkled on each table. Simple but beautiful bouquets of lilies and lavender exuded a subtle, sweet fragrance as we walked by, but I barely noticed. The band played a soft melody as the waitstaff quietly weaved through the crowd handing out champagne. Fritz grabbed two full glasses with one hand as he forced me into a chair.

"Now wait a minute," a deep voice behind me said. "I barely got to kiss my bride before I got jacked in the balls, and now someone else is trying to make a toast without me? I don't think so." Michael stepped in, slapping Fritz on the back with a lopsided grin.

"Emily," he said, looking at me with those gorgeous blue eyes, "babe, what's going on?" He set his ice pack down and took my hands in his, a slightly pained look on his face. I felt myself immediately began to relax at his touch. I loved this man.

"My dad was here. He was *here,* Michael. And he left me this note. I know it sounds crazy, but it's true." I showed him the bits that remained, the paper disintegrating before my eyes. Was this some kind of super biodegradable paper? I'd never seen paper turn to mush this quickly. "Well, it was a note before it hit the water. And it was from him. I know it. It was *his* handwriting, Michael. *His.*"

The look Michael gave me was full of love and tenderness...and a little bit of doubt. After all, my dad had been dead for almost two years. I explained how Father McDermott had found me after the ceremony and given me the note just before I fainted at the sight of it.

"I need to find Father. If we can find him, he might be able to lead me to my dad. He saw him. He spoke to him!"

"Emily, hon, just hold on." I could see him struggle to find the right words. "Why do you think the person who spoke to Father was your dad? I mean, it could have been anyone. Everyone who knows you knows your parents died under mysterious circumstances." He paused, looking around at the crowd before facing me again. "The fraud case dealing with the estate was all over the news. Anyone could have read that and followed us out here from Texas, trying to mess with you in hopes of getting some of your money. I just—"

"Michael," I interrupted, "the note was from my dad. I have no doubt about it. No one can copy chicken scratch like that. I know it was him!"

Michael sat still for a few beats, his brow knitted in confusion. He looked at Fritz, who simply shrugged. I could tell Michael was planning his words carefully. He remained completely calm, while I was practically jumping out of my skin.

"I just think you shouldn't jump to conclusions yet, babe. It's our wedding day. Our celebration." He gave me a sad smile and continued. "Let's try to find Father and get to the bottom of this. This person claiming to be your dad...why didn't he stay? If it really is your dad, why has he been hiding for almost two years, only to appear at our wedding and leave again? We also have to remember we have 100 guests here, waiting to celebrate with us. We've got to approach this rationally. We can't just go off on a wild goose chase when we literally said our vows thirty minutes ago. Come," he said, brushing my cheek with his hand, "celebrate with me."

I looked around at the tables full of our friends and family. Many of the sorority girls from the college where I was a former house mom had come out to California for the wedding. My good friends Tom and Joan, who I considered family, had driven up from their new home. The majority of our guests were from Michael's huge family, but I didn't mind. They were so loving and had welcomed me and made me feel like one of their own from the very beginning.

"You're right," I said, dropping my head. I sighed, trying not to get ahead of myself, but I was completely obsessed with the glimmer of hope that my dad might actually be alive. "I'm going to get cleaned up. You go find Father. We'll get this figured out. But for now," I said, swallowing and pasting on a smile, "we celebrate." Michael and I picked up our glasses of champagne, made a toast, and swallowed them down in one gulp. People started clinking their glasses with their forks, shouting, "Kiss! Kiss!", and we happily obliged. I felt my body began to turn to mush as I kissed him, and I wished for a brief second that we could both slip out and find a private room for ourselves.

• CHAPTER 3 •

I GOT UP AND SLIPPED OUT to the bathroom instead, hoping to clean myself off a little bit more before mingling with guests. No one wants to chat with a bride who has particles of sand and tiny crustaceans falling out of her hair.

I knew Michael would find Father, and I knew Father would lead us to this person who may or may not be my dad. But I didn't know how I would force myself to act as if everything were normal until then. How was any of this normal?

The bathrooms were located just uphill from the beach in the resort where most of the guests were staying. I found the outdoor shower just outside the building and went to rinse off my legs and feet. Luckily, my wedding dress was a simple chiffon sheath, and I could hold my skirt in one hand, unlike the heavy Cinderella ball gowns some brides opted for. I slid my feet under the cool spray of the water, feeling relief as the itchy sand rinsed off my legs.

"Hey girl, you okay?" Lisa slipped up from behind, putting her arm around me. "Geez, I didn't expect you to be rolling around in the sand until you'd had at least three strong cocktails in you." She smiled at me with a question in her eyes. "Really. Is everything okay?"

Lisa had been my BFF since seventh grade when my family had moved to Houston, my former home. She befriended me as an awkward teenager with braces, frizzy hair, and a "Yankee accent" (according to them) in that oh-so-Southern town. She's the sister I never had, and the one who kept me going when my parents died suddenly not so long ago. Well, at least, I thought they had died. Everything I'd known to be true was up in the air now.

"Yeah, everything all right?" Carley said, stumbling up behind Lisa in her three-inch stilettos. Carley Rae McSchatz had been one of my sorority sisters back in college; the biggest partying bow-head of them all. Ten-plus years later, she had tamed down, wizened up, and dropped the middle name, and was now the sole owner of a very successful salon. We'd reconnected last year when I'd had to move back to my old college town to keep from being homeless. "You've done a number on your hair. Good thing I know someone that might be able to fix it." She winked, and together with Lisa, helped me up the steps into the resort's luxury bathrooms.

I didn't know what to say to them. Should I tell them what happened? Would they believe me? Likely not. I barely believed it myself. I didn't even think my new husband believed me. And Fritz certainly thought I was nuts. But what's new about that? I saw what I saw and I knew what I knew...I thought.

Walking into the bathroom, which came complete with a full sitting area, television, and minibar (Really? Aren't we in the bathroom because we've had a little too much of that already?), I made up my mind. Startling both girls by turning around to lock the door behind us, I took a deep breath and filled them in.

"Omigod," Lisa said a few minutes later, dumbstruck. "Omigod, Em. I always knew your dad was a spy. I knew it!"

"He's not a spy, Lisa! Geez! He's just alive, apparently. Maybe. I hope." I couldn't believe I was saying those words.

"Um, hello?! Why would he be alive and not contact you for almost two years if he's not in hiding for some reason? Why the hell would he show up at your wedding and *leave*? And why would he be in hiding if he's not a spy?"

About a year ago, I found out that my BFF had lived under the illusion that my dad was a secret agent for, apparently, most of the time she had known me. My dad had been an entrepreneur all of his adult life. While one of his deals had gotten him into trouble just before he died—or rather, maybe didn't die, I guess—he'd never been in trouble before. He never had secret rendezvous with operatives. He had always been a constant presence in my life, except when he was traveling on business trips. Which were pretty frequent...and always last minute. And I never really knew exactly what he was doing. But, no! I refused to believe he was a spy. He was just a dad! *My* dad! Completely harmless and innocent, except for this reappearing out of nowhere thing...

"I don't know, Lisa. I don't know anything!"

"What about your mom? Was she here too?"

"I don't think so. Her name wasn't on the note, and Father just said a man handed it to him. He didn't mention anything about a female companion. I don't know where my mom is. But if he's still alive, surely she is too." I hoped I was right.

"Michael is trying to find Father and I'm supposed to get cleaned up so we can continue with the reception before we investigate further. Only I don't know how I can do that. I'm freaking out!"

"Of course you are. Who wouldn't be?" Carley agreed and reached into her purse and pulled out a mini hair dryer. "Always prepared," she said in response to my startled look. "Now hold still while I blow this sand out of your hair real quick. Then we can figure out how to find your dad."

The hot air hit me and I flipped my head over, letting Carley shake the sand out of my hair. I studied my long, light brown hair as it fell in waves, thankful for the recent highlights that now glistened in the harsh fluorescent light. Lisa gently wiped sand off my arms and back, and I shook off my dress, taking care not to shake loose any of the beading lightly scattered around the skirt.

"Well, really, you shouldn't jump to conclusions yet," Lisa yelled over the hum of the dryer.

"That's just what Michael said!" I exclaimed.

"And he's right. This whole thing could be a spoof. Tonight is your night. You just got *married*! Celebrate it! If the person who spoke to Father really is your dad, he's been hiding for almost two years. He's let everyone in the world think he and your mom are dead. He left you high and dry when his estate was almost taken away from you. He let you almost get killed trying to get it back and defend his honor. Then he comes to your wedding and leaves before you can see him? Something's not right with that. Any of that. He can wait. I'm sorry, but he can wait."

Lisa crossed her arms and went silent. I brought my head back up and could see the anger emanating off her, tears forming in her bright green eyes. Carley turned off the hair dryer and pulled out a curling wand and hairspray from her seemingly bottomless purse.

"If your dad's been hanging around these past two years while you have suffered so much...well, I'm sorry, but I'm gonna have to kick his ass." Lisa's body was shaking as she tried to keep her emotions in check, and a tear slid down her cheek.

"I have to agree, Emily," Carley said. She began to curl random sections of my hair with ease. Steam radiated off the curler, and I got a brief whiff of seaweed. "I never knew your dad, but if he's still alive and hasn't been in touch, that's not cool. And illegal. You can't be declared dead and keep on living somewhere else. Whether it's him or someone else impersonating him, why don't you have Fritz look into it?" She put the curler down, tied my hair back in a loose ponytail at the nape of my neck, pulled a few tendrils loose, and began to spray. "That's his specialty. And that way you and Michael can celebrate your honeymoon, knowing things are in good hands. Fritz will get things settled. You know he will." She continued to coif my hair and reapply my makeup with ease. Thank God for this woman. I would look like a peasant without her.

I thought about what she said. I had hired Carley's Uncle Fritz late last year to help me sort out my dad's estate when he'd been accused of fraud and all assets were frozen after his (supposed?) death. As a private investigator, Fritz had access to all kinds of information it would have taken me years to get. He'd helped me find the people responsible for nearly bilking my dad out of all of his money in a night I will never forget.

I was convinced Fritz could find anyone and anything. He was the obvious choice to look for my dad. I just had to convince him that the note was real and I wasn't out of my mind first. And I had to hope he wasn't already committed to another case.

"Good idea, Carley." I was beginning to feel like I had things under control already. "I will talk to Fritz and see what he says."

"Whoa. Uh, you'd better talk to Michael first," Lisa said, sniffing and fanning her eyes to dry her tears. "Remember the last time you worked with Fritz." Lisa was referring to the night in which I found out who had tried to cheat my dad and ruin his legacy and had nearly died proving it.

"Of course I will talk to Michael first." I looked in the mirror and wiped my hands lightly over my face and arms one more time. "We're a married couple now. All decisions like this should be made together." I turned around and gave both of them a smile to seal the deal, deciding it was time to head back outside to face the crowd and Michael. I knew Michael would support me in anything Fritz might want to do in order to find my dad if he was, indeed, alive. At least, I hoped he would. *After all, there won't be any guns and hostage holding this time,* I thought to myself. Right? Well, I'd certainly make sure of it.

• CHAPTER 4 •

THE GIRLS AND I made a pact not to speak of things again until after the reception when Michael and I had decided on a plan of action. Our guests didn't need to know the full extent of what had gone on. For now, we were telling everyone that I had just become light-headed and fainted, and that my vows nearly got swallowed up by the ocean.

Now I just had to find Michael and square things away with him. He was easy to find, as he stands about a head taller than most people. I spotted his sandy-blond hair right away, nicely trimmed up for the wedding. He was looking all gorgeous in his tuxedo, standing casually by a table filled with his family, laughing at something. A grin lit up his face. My heart skipped a beat, and I couldn't help but smile.

"Hey, you," I said, walking up and putting my arms around his waist. He turned his face to me and the clinking of the glasses began again, turning his small peck into a deep, lingering kiss. I didn't mind at all but found myself blushing.

"Did you find out anything?" I asked quietly when we came up for air. "Did you find Father McDermott?"

"No such luck, and I'm afraid we won't be able to speak to him for a while." He took my arm and led me away from the table toward the stage. "I'll explain in a minute. Right now, Shaniqua says we have to say something and make a toast." He glanced up at our wedding coordinator, who was motioning at the two of us. Tall, dark, and beautiful, Shaniqua was a force to be reckoned with, and that's how she ran events such as this so smoothly. "People have been clamoring for an announcement of some sort so they can raid the food line. We've got a bunch of hungry people here, and my nephews aren't going to be able to sit still much longer."

As one of seven children, Michael has a host of nieces and nephews ranging from age two to twenty-two. The smaller children were running amok on the beach, under the watchful eye of their older siblings. I looked around and noticed that all of the appetizers had indeed been devoured, and only empty dishes remained. It was late in the day, and I got a strong sense that we'd have a small riot on our hands if people weren't fed a proper meal soon.

"Okay, that makes sense. People are hungry and need to be fed. Let's start the line." I headed over to the buffet, enticed by the smells of roasted chicken and smoked salmon. As I eyed the immense amount of decadent food, I realized for the first time all day that I was starving.

"Hold on there," Michael said, stopping me. "Not quite yet. We've got to make announcements. You know, thank people for coming. Tell them how overjoyed we are at being married. Invite them to enjoy themselves all evening with us. Well," he started, getting a sly grin on his face and nibbling my ear, "all evening meaning the next couple of hours. Then it's just you and me and a nice king-sized bed...or maybe we take a tumble in the sand if you'd prefer. Ooh, or even an isolated cave in the water. Or maybe a hot tub. Or maybe all of the above." He wiggled his eyebrows. "Damn," he continued, taking a deep breath and slowly exhaling. "I need a cold shower. This could get embarrassing quick."

As my poor husband struggled to think innocent thoughts and compose himself, I squeezed his arm, then walked onstage myself, eager to get things going. I had a word with Shaniqua, and a minute later, Michael joined me, fully able to stand upright without creating a scene.

We went to the microphone and thanked everyone for coming and joining us on our amazing wedding day. I made a joke about fainting at the thought of no longer being a single lady. Michael said he hoped he'd be as much fun to live with as ten sorority girls. It was hard to believe that was my life just a few short months ago, but I was overjoyed about what lay ahead.

Once the toasts were finished, we headed to the buffet line. I was eager to pepper Michael with questions about why we might not be able to speak to Father for a while.

"Spill it," I whispered to him, taking a plate and asking the server for roasted chicken.

"Well, it's not what you want to hear—"

"Oh honey, you look gorgeous!" my mother-in-law interrupted, appearing behind me. Tall, slender, and regal looking, you'd never have guessed this woman had given birth to, and raised, so many children. "You poor thing. You take a tumble in the sand, but twenty minutes later, you look as good as new." Michael nearly spat out the piece of salmon he had snatched from his plate.

"You took a tumble without me?" he mouthed as I stifled a giggle.

"Well, thank you," I said to his mom, trying my best to ignore him. "The fainting was unexpected. I'm hoping for a more uneventful evening from here on out." I continued down the line as the servers piled my dish high with vegetables and potatoes.

"I should hope uneventful isn't what you're going for," she continued without looking at me. "It is your wedding night, after all." A small smile played at the corners of her mouth, and I found myself once again blushing. And speechless. Awkward!

She continued talking. "Boy, I sure am glad Father was able to squeeze the wedding in before he left." Stopping at the bread bowl and considering her choices, she settled on whole grain. "A silent, three-week retreat to the Holy Land!" she exclaimed. "No cell service, no email. Why, I think we should all do that once in our lives. And to fly out just after celebrating a wedding! The man must be exhausted. Good thing he has a long flight. Hope he gets some sleep on the plane.

"Are you done, dear?" She paused and looked at my plate as I stood there, unable to move. "You must really like bread."

I looked down at my plate to see a mound of food covered with six rolls. I had totally lost track of what I was doing when she blindsided me with the fact that the only person who may have seen my dad was now on a plane to Jerusalem, of all places, unreachable for the next three weeks!

Panicked, I looked over at Michael. He nodded with a frown. "See what I mean?" he said. "Not what you wanted to hear."

I managed to eat my plateful of food, sans the six rolls (I ate two and Michael took the rest), while trying to act as if everything was completely fine. Michael kept squeezing my hand under the table, whispering that it would all work out. We made it through several more toasts, one roast from his nephew Matt, whom I adore, and a lot of hugs and tears. It was a beautiful evening. The cool, crisp breeze swirled around us, the smell of the ocean filled the air, and the waves quietly pounded behind us. It was an incredible time shared with friends and family. Except for the mystery of my parents' whereabouts, everything was perfect. However, I could not shake the anxious feeling that I knew would consume me until I had answers. Still, I did my best to enjoy the evening. How many of my own wedding receptions would I get to experience, after all? I hoped just this one.

Michael and I mingled with our guests, laughing and telling stories of what brought us together; how when I first met Michael, I made a good impression by whacking him in the head with a door.

"I thought you had broken into my house," I said in my defense. "What's a girl to do? But you still fell in love with me anyway." I smiled. "Well, maybe not right away..."

Several of my former sorority girls were in attendance, and they giggled over who they thought would catch the bouquet.

"I'm staying as far away from that as I can," said Maria, by far the most fiercely independent of the group. But it didn't stop her from scanning all of the attractive males in attendance from head to toe. I loved Maria and her take-charge attitude.

"Ooh, I want it! I can't wait to get married!" Candy said. "But then that means I need to find a boyfriend first..." Candy's last relationship hadn't ended so well. Her ex-boyfriend, Shiner, was the one who had tried to take my dad's money and had held both her and me hostage while he raged about the unfairness of possibly losing all that cash. Thankfully, he was now in jail.

Michelle just stood there, smiling and not saying anything. Instead, she watched her boyfriend, Chris, play with Michael's nieces and nephews, a little twinkle in her eye.

All three of those girls had graduated the previous spring and were still getting used to life after undergrad. They didn't know yet where life would take them, but I knew we'd all manage to stay in touch. We'd gone through too much in the past year not to.

Before I knew it, the band started up again, and it was time for the first dance. While we'd been mingling, I'd been thinking a little bit about just how we could get to Father sooner than three weeks from now. I was desperate to find out more information about my dad. I had come up with a little plan that would require a slight detour before our honeymoon and just had to convince Michael it was the right thing to do. But I wasn't at all certain that I could.

Acting as the master of ceremonies, Shaniqua got things going by introducing the band and welcoming Michael and me onto the small, temporary dance floor for our first dance. She had everything completely under control, having done this very thing hundreds of times for clients, and I felt better knowing it. Lights glittered around us as the crowd hushed and the band began to strum the first chords of an old Dixie Chicks song I had picked in homage to Michael's Texas roots. Michael took me in his arms and held me close, his warm breath in my ear. I could feel his solid muscles through his tuxedo shirt, his heart beating against my own chest. He took my hand and tilted his head down so that his lips hovered just over mine as we began to dance to the music.

"Are you having a nice time, Mrs. Drake?" he whispered. "Or would you prefer I whisk you away from here to someplace we can be alone? Maybe a nice, secluded resort nestled in the mountains?" He grinned and his lips touched mine just briefly, teasing me. My breath became shallow and my body wanted to melt into his. I knew I had to say something about my plan before I completely lost my ability to think clearly. After all, we were leaving for Colorado in the morning, and tickets had to be changed. But right now, I could only focus on my husband and his body touching mine.

I swallowed and pushed my lewd thoughts to the back of my head, promising myself I'd get this over with quickly and make it as painless as possible.

"I cannot wait to get to the mountains." I smiled, looking up at him with my best puppy dog eyes. "But I'd feel so much better if we could get something settled first." I felt Michael tense up just a bit, but I forged on. "I think that I just wouldn't be able to put all of my focus on our honeymoon if I was still wondering about my parents." Michael nearly went still. This wasn't going so well. "I think maybe we could just take a quick detour to the Holy Land before we go to Colorado, speak to Father, maybe see a few sights, and then be on our way. That way I'd have some peace of mind and—"

"We are *not* having our first fight as a married couple at our wedding reception," Michael said with a forced grin.

"Smile for the camera!" The photographer interrupted us from out of nowhere, blinding us with her flash. We complied and gave her our biggest smiles, hoping no one would notice the mounting tension between us.

"Then don't disagree with me," I joked with Michael, trying to lighten the mood. "We can hop on a plane to Jerusalem, find Father in the Holy Land, and be back to enjoy a few days in the Rockies."

"You don't just 'hop on a plane to Jerusalem' and then cruise on over to Colorado. You're turning a two-hour flight into a forty-eight-hour nightmare." He paused and closed his eyes briefly, clearly trying to contain his building frustration. "Besides, we are not spending any time on our honeymoon in the Holy Land." Michael stared into my eyes, his face relaxing and his gaze intense with longing. "I plan on doing lots of unholy things to and with you while we are on our honeymoon, and it wouldn't be appropriate." I'd been holding my breath waiting for his response and found I was becoming dizzy at his words. He started nuzzling my neck, his five o'clock shadow gently grazing my skin. I closed my eyes briefly and let out a sigh, letting my mind wander for just a bit, a smile playing at my lips. When I looked up, I was startled and embarrassed to see his mom's gaze fixed on me, one eyebrow raised.

"Michael," I giggled, "you need to stop it!" I made a half-assed attempt to pull away. "Your parents are watching."

"It's called the art of seduction, Emily. My parents know all about what's going on. They do have seven kids, you know." He kept tracing kisses up my neck.

"Oh, you are disgusting," I joked. "Parents don't have sex. My parents only did once...and they didn't enjoy it." Lisa and I had always said this growing up, refusing to believe that our parents could be sexual beings.

"Okay, babe. Whatever you say." Michael's low voice whispered in my ear, making my knees weak. "Well, except for going to the Holy Land. We are not doing that. I have much more fun things planned..." I snuggled deeper into him as he whispered just what he had in mind for our honeymoon, letting his strong arms keep me standing as my body melted at his words. How much longer was this reception?

• CHAPTER 5 •

TRUE TO HIS WORD, Michael didn't let me change our tickets to fly to Colorado via Jerusalem. But we did agree I'd speak to Fritz about trying to contact Father McDermott while we were gone. Hopefully he could get a bead on my dad or the person impersonating him.

"I'll try to get in touch with Father through some connections I have in Israel," Fritz said, "but I'm not heading over to the Holy Land. Good God, I'd burn up upon entry for sure!"

Fritz grilled me for a while to get anything he could that might help him get a bead on my dad, but in his mind, he was certain it was a hoax. "I have a very strong feeling that someone is just messing with you, kid." He frowned and squeezed my arm. "Just don't get your hopes up too much, okay?" Still, he agreed to look through some of his magical databases and put out feelers. I knew that if there was anything to be found, Fritz was the man to find it.

Fritz had been an enormous help in flushing out the two guys that had made a crooked deal with my dad before his death. While I hadn't known him for long, he'd become a great friend to both Michael and me and had recently played a key role in my life. He had even refused payment for his services the first time we worked together, saying he'd had far too much fun with it to charge me. Plus, he'd done quite well at the poker tables by the time he had left New Orleans, the place it all went down. This time I let him know in advance that there were no more freebies. Now that my trust fund was back in place, I had plenty of money to cover his fees.

The rest of our wedding reception was spent dancing, talking with friends and family, and performing all of the usual wedding traditions. Michelle caught the bouquet, her tall frame easily towering several inches over all the other ladies. Her boyfriend Chris had caught the garter, and the crowd whooped with joy at the thought of those two being the next couple to walk down the aisle.

After a couple of hours and increasingly provocative comments from my husband, we were both antsy to take our leave. The reception had been a great celebration of the beautiful marriage we had begun, but Michael flat out told me he was horny and it was time to go. I didn't argue.

I had already made plans with Maria and Candy to house sit while we went on our honeymoon. They would help out at the antique store I now owned and stay at our house in La Jolla, watching over my cat, Daisy. Neither of them had full time jobs yet, so they were happy for the additional cash, and I was happy for the help. Plus, our house, though a fixer-upper and not in the best shape, was only a ten-minute walk to the beach. It was win-win for all parties involved.

We didn't bother with a limo, and instead rented a sporty convertible that Michael's nieces and nephews had decorated with shoe polish, streamers, and tin cans. Michael revved the engine as we departed, and we waved at our guests as they disappeared on the horizon, twirling sparklers, blowing kisses, and wishing us well.

"So, Mrs. Drake, are you ready for this?" Michael grabbed my hand and kissed it before setting it in his lap. My hair, now loose, whipped around my head as he drove. "Are you ready to spend eternity by my side?"

"You bet I am." Trying to snuggle closer to him, I felt something press into my gut and pulled back in surprise. Looking down, I laughed. "Hmmm, is that a gear shift, or are you happy to see me?" I leaned back into him. I slowly ran my hand up his thigh and softly began kissing his cheek, tracing a line down his neck. His cologne had a subtle, woody scent, and his skin was warm under my lips.

"Oh boy," he groaned, shifting gears with a screech. "Watch it there. You don't want me to crash this thing before we even get to the B&B, do you?" He laughed huskily. *"Focus, Michael, focus. Five more miles. Five more miles."* His foot pressed down hard on the accelerator, and the car raced easily along the winding ocean-side road.

I continued to tease him as he drove, careful not to go too far. I couldn't believe how lucky I was to have this gorgeous, strong, hardworking, loving man as my husband. Forever.

We reached the B&B in no time, barely putting the car in park before we both jumped out and raced each other to the door. "Wait," Michael said breathlessly, pulling me back, just as I tried to enter. "I have to carry you over the threshold."

"Aw, if you insist." Wrapping my arms around his neck, I let him lift me as if I weighed nothing at all and carry me into the cottage.

A giant display of white roses greeted us, along with chilled champagne and a small fountain of flowing chocolate with strawberries on the side. Candles twinkled in their holders and a ceiling fan spun lazily overhead.

"Oh wow, this looks amazing!" I said, taking it all in. The B&B was a stand-alone, one-room cottage, with the back wall made entirely of windows offering a sweeping view of the ocean. The hostess had left several of the windows open, and a light breeze floated in, giving me goosebumps.

Michael set me down but held me close. "You don't get to leave my arms all night," he said, softly kissing my lips.

"Okay," I answered, slipping my arms through his. "No complaints here."

He slowly began undoing the buttons on the back of my dress as I slid my hands down to his hips, pulling him closer.

"I cannot wait to get you—"

Suddenly, a shrill ring pierced through the air, causing us both to jump back in surprise.

"What the—?!" Michael exclaimed in frustration. "Are you kidding me?" He reached into his pocket and grabbed his cell phone, put it on mute, and threw it on the bedside table. "Damn phone!" My heart was racing, and I did a physical assessment to make sure I hadn't peed my pants. Who would be calling us on our wedding night? Could it be about my dad?

"Now, where was I?" He took ahold of my face and drew closer.

"Wait, don't you want to see who it was?" I asked breathlessly between kisses. "What if Fritz has—? What if it's impor—? Michael!"

Michael stopped and took a deep breath, his gaze intense with heat. "I don't give a damn who it is or what is going on anywhere but right here, right now, with you, inside this room, or outside on the balcony, the beach, the water, wherever." He looked into my eyes, his lips again grazing mine, and my body again responded instantly. "I have only one thing in mind, babe, and anything else can wait." He silenced me with another kiss, and I willingly succumbed. In that moment, the world could have been falling down right around us, and I wouldn't have cared one tiny bit.

• CHAPTER 6 •

OUR WEDDING NIGHT was amazing...and I'll just leave it at that. The B&B hostess thankfully does not live on site, and she dropped off a lavish breakfast for us at a prearranged time. We fed each other fruit and buttery, chocolate-filled pastries out on the balcony overlooking the deep blue ocean. Seals sunned themselves on a large rock just off the beach in the distance. The beauty of this part of the country never ceased to amaze me.

I found myself wondering if we could ever own a place like this someday. I knew that even with our combined incomes and my trust fund, we couldn't afford an oceanfront house unless we spent every penny, but just thinking about it was a way to keep my mind off of obsessing about my dad. Was Fritz having any luck finding

Father? Had Father even landed in Jerusalem yet? It was all out of my hands right now but, despite our amazing night, my mind was racing and I had to work hard at relaxing.

I looked over at my husband lounging on the deck, staring at the ocean, his brow slightly furrowed. He'd checked his messages earlier and had seemed slightly distracted ever since. I knew he was trying to distance himself from work for our honeymoon, and I debated asking him about it. He had a few big construction projects lined up, but his crew knew how important it was for him to be completely hands off for a few days.

"Is everything okay? At work, I mean?" I asked hesitantly, grabbing his hand. "Can they survive a few days without you?"

"What? Why do you ask?" A puzzled look crossed his face as he turned to face me.

"The phone call last night? Wasn't that from the crew?" Who else would call on a person's wedding night unless it was an emergency?

"Oh, yeah, that call." He sighed deeply, avoiding my gaze. "That's taken care of. Don't worry about it." His face told me he was irritated at the memory of it, and I felt bad for asking.

"Well good. I'm sure they'll be able to handle everything while you're gone. They know you need some time to relax." He gave me a wry grin and nodded. I decided to change the subject.

Looking around the secluded property, I fantasized about living in such a place. All of the worries from a stressful day would be forgotten once you stepped on out on the back deck with this gorgeous view of the ocean.

"What would it take to get a place like this? Besides a few million dollars..." I wondered aloud. "This is really all the space we need."

"Well, yeah, sure, but...what about kids?" Michael asked, yawning and stretching his legs out on the chaise.

"What about them?"

"There's no room for kids here. At all. We'd have to add on."

That was true, seeing as it was a one-room cottage. "Well, you could do that easily, couldn't you?" I asked my contractor husband, still fantasizing. A project like this would be nothing compared to what he usually worked on. "Besides, why are you worried about kids already?" I wasn't worried about kids. I had other things on my mind right now. Namely, solving this mystery of my father. *Must work on thinking of other things. Serenity now. Serenity now.* I tried deep breathing.

"I'm not *worried* about kids. I'm just saying we don't have enough room here. But," he said, looking around at the landscape, shrugging his shoulders, "this is a large piece of land. We could expand. Maybe add another living space, a big kitchen, five or six more bedrooms."

"*Five or six more bedrooms?*" I laughed, turning to face him. "How many kids are you expecting us to have?"

"Well, I don't know." He paused and stroked his chin. "But I have a great idea." He looked at me with a sexy grin. "Why don't we go ahead and get started? Or at least practice some more. Because, you know, practice makes perfect." He reached over and pulled me into his lap, gently wiped a crumb from my cheek, and kissed me hungrily. "Hmmm...we haven't christened the balcony yet..."

Sometime later we disentangled from each other and decided we were going to miss our flight if we didn't get moving in a different way. I reluctantly left Michael to take a quick shower before getting ready. I walked into the bathroom and stared in the mirror. What I saw was a woman whose face was flush with love and physical satisfaction. I was so grateful for what I had. With Michael, my friends, my new business...my life was abundantly full. To have my parents possibly alive and back in my life...well, I couldn't even express the kind of joy that would bring.

I sighed and began to unpack my toiletries, putting all other thoughts aside and focusing on getting ready. I told Michael I would leave it in Fritz's capable hands for the next seven days, and I would not break my promise. Or I'd at least try my best. Starting now. Michael's voice carried from the other room as I laid things out in the posh bathroom. He had said he had one call to make, just some loose ends he'd forgotten to tie up. His deep voice sounded concerned, and I hoped his ongoing projects would be okay without him. I wanted his complete attention on our honeymoon, not a distracted, worried husband. I swear, sometimes I'm such a hypocrite.

As the shower warmed up and steam began to fill the room, I opened the door and got in. I had turned on the dual shower heads to warm things up more quickly and luxuriated in the scalding hot water, my muscles turning to putty in my self-made sauna. I let the jets pound on my shoulders, feeling the tension begin to wash away. After a few moments, a brief cool breeze wafted over my skin and I opened my eyes to see Michael standing before me, a big smile on his face and his pleasure...evident.

"There are two shower heads for a reason, Emily. I can't believe you'd try to shower without me." He got in and pulled me close, his mouth coming down over mine. This would never get old.

• CHAPTER 7 •

THE FLIGHT TO DENVER wasn't too long, thankfully, even from San Diego. However, I felt it necessary to drink a salty Bloody Mary because a) we were in first class, and it was free, so why not? And, b) so I would not have to use the airplane bathroom at all, if I could help it. My plan worked, but my feet also swelled up so much I could barely put my flip-flops back on once we landed.

Denver is a booming metropolis. The airport and traffic are crazy busy, but the Rocky Mountains are only about ninety minutes away by car. Navigating the airport and heavily traveled roads to get to that gorgeous destination would be worth it. It's not much different than the craziness of Houston and San Diego, and we would have a view of the mountains in front of us the whole way. Plus, Michael was going to drive. All I had to do was sit back and enjoy the scenery.

As we departed the plane, we headed to baggage claim and then the rental car counter. Once we got settled with all of our bags (thank God—a minor miracle in this day and age) and our rental (a midsize, neon green 4WD SUV for off-roading), we set out to map our way to the resort. This entailed the tedious process of entering the resort's address into our phone's mapping app and hitting "Go". Quite different from when I was a kid and my dad would awkwardly hand my mom a map the size of the front seat and ask her to navigate.

Once we got on the road and headed west, the view of the mountains became clearer and clearer. I hadn't been to this part of the country since I was a kid. The Rockies had been one of my parents' favorite destinations, and we'd come here every summer until we moved to Houston. It seemed only fitting, since Michael and I currently lived in the tropical paradise of La Jolla, that we enjoy a different kind of scenery for our first week as a married couple. In fact, we'd planned on a week at the B&B in La Jolla. Moving expenses and the cost of setting up both of our new businesses had made me hesitant to spend even more money on a lavish honeymoon. But then, as luck would have it, I won a honeymoon stay at a luxury resort in Elkston, Colorado, from a contest I'd entered on a whim. I saw it as a sign that we were meant to come to this place. We both agreed that we get enough palm trees and sun at home, so we opted for a romantic getaway in the mountains instead. I was so excited to breathe the cool, crisp, fresh mountain air. There is nothing else like it.

I gazed out the windows as the landscape slowly changed as we gained altitude. We drove with the windows down to get as much of the fresh air as we could. The smell of rain was in the air, probably from a late afternoon thunderstorm, which are very common in that area. I reached over and held Michael's hand as he drove.

"Hey, no messing around with me while I'm driving today, okay?" he joked. "As much as I'd love it, I have to navigate winding mountain roads." He frowned. "I can't believe I'm saying this, but save that for later." He blew me a kiss and put both hands on the steering wheel.

"Fine," I sighed, keeping my hand still on his thigh. Immediately, I felt his phone begin to vibrate through his pocket. "Do you want me to get that for you?"

He was quick to answer. "Nope. Whoever it is can wait."

"You sure?"

"Positive. We're officially on our honeymoon. No work calls allowed."

"What if it's Fritz?"

"Babe, I don't think there's any way Father could even be in Jerusalem yet. That's a long day of flying and layovers for him. No way Fritz has gotten in touch with him."

"But what if he's—"

"Emily, be patient. You promised..." he gently reminded me. "Besides, if Fritz had any new info, don't you think he'd be calling you instead of me? Is your phone ringing?"

He had a point, but just to be sure, I checked my phone one more time. No new messages or calls, but I noticed my battery was getting low.

I sighed and continued to focus on the beauty of our surroundings. Flat ranchland turned into low, rolling hills as we continued northwest. Gaining elevation, more and more rocky outcrops began to pop up. Sage brush replaced leafy bushes, and pine trees and aspen dotted the foothills. Small businesses selling local wares were scattered throughout the countryside.

I distracted myself by talking with Michael about what hikes we would want to take. He had been to the Rockies before, but only in the winter as a kid for downhill skiing and snowboarding. He'd never been hiking in the mountains, and the competitive side of me was eager to see which one of us would succumb to altitude sickness and sore feet sooner. We decided to start off with some easier hikes to give our bodies some time to get used to the altitude, and work our way up to the larger peaks and maybe even the tougher 14ers, if we got that far.

As we climbed higher into the mountains, the sun began to set and my stomach growled, reminding me that we hadn't eaten real food in several hours. Thankfully, we soon reached the resort. Driving on those winding roads, with the mountains towering up on either side of us as it neared dark, was a bit unnerving. We pulled up to the circle drive where the valet offered to check us in, take our bags to our private cabin, and park the car so we could head to the restaurant to eat.

The resort was luxurious and rustic at the same time. It consisted of a main lodge and several private cabins that dotted the mountainside, all with sweeping views of the Rockies. Or at least, I knew as much from the travel agent. It was twilight when we arrived, so we had a sweeping view of...impending darkness and tall pine trees. The walk to the restaurant solidified the idea that we were in a lush resort. All of the finishes were high end, and you could easily tell much care went into the planning and design. Each cabin area was lush and secluded enough to create a sense of privacy without being totally isolated. The landscape was dotted with local flowers and shrubbery, twinkling lanterns, and towering pines. Everything looked impeccably maintained.

We followed a winding trail to the log cabin-esque restaurant, and opted to sit out on the patio, immediately ordering two local brews while perusing the menu. The view as the sun dipped below the mountaintops was stunning. The national park entrance was only a few miles away, and we were surrounded by mountains. A herd of elk grazed in the distance, barely visible in the light of the setting sun. Heat lamps were scattered around the patio as the temperature quickly plummeted. Luckily, we had pulled our jackets out of our luggage before leaving our car with the valet, and I quickly put mine on, wishing I had thought to grab my hat.

"I forgot how chilly it can get here at night, especially this time of year," I remarked, rubbing my hands together.

"Probably why we're the only ones out here," Michael added with a smile. "I don't mind though. I like being alone with my bride."

He took my hand and kissed it, sending shivers up my spine. Or maybe that was the fifty-degree temps. I scooted closer to him and he slid his arm around me, nuzzling the side of my face. My body instantly began to warm up, and I smiled.

"Mind if we join y'all?"

Startled, we both turned around to see a couple that screamed "Texas" walking onto the patio. It might be my astonishing powers of observation or the fact that the guy wore a ten-gallon hat and a belt buckle the size of his fist with a rendering of the state and the word "TEXAS" boldly written across it, that gave it away. He was very muscular, his biceps practically busting out of the tight T-shirt he was wearing. I might have been staring, as I felt a not-so-gentle nudge under the table. I quickly averted my eyes to his companion.

His wife, or girlfriend, had giant Texas hair, bleached blonde and curled within an inch of its life. Her tight sweater accentuated her curvy figure and I could sense my other half doing his own share of staring. I nudged him right back. The light mountain breeze that gently tousled my hair didn't budge hers one bit. We always referred to that as "helmet head" in high school, and I'm the first to admit I went through my own Aqua Net phase trying to fit in. I have long since packed any evidence of that far, far away, never to be seen again. I hope.

"Of course!" Michael and I said as the couple walked to the table right next to us, the woman setting her purse down. Michael raised the one eyebrow and gave me a lopsided grin as he glanced around at the other ten or so empty tables scattered farther away around the patio. So much for being alone.

"Boy, it is just frigid out here, y'all!" the woman exclaimed. "But I told Dirk, 'We're up north now. We gotta take in this winter weather while we can!' So we're gonna sit out here and have us some hot cocoa.

"Baby, will you run back up to the room and grab my parka? It's just darn near freezing out here! Brrrrr!" she said with a shiver, squeezing her arms around her bosom, nearly popping her boobs out of her V-neck sweater.

"You hang right in there, baby," Dirk said. "Go on and stand by one of them there heaters. Go on now. Daddy's gonna warm you right up," he said, pinching her bottom. "Be back in two shakes."

Dirk went back inside, presumably to find them some coats, scarves, gloves, and hats. I wanted to ask him to bring me something too. The woman warmed herself up by the large heat lamp right between our two tables. She towered over Michael as he sat, and I glanced down at the three-inch boots she was wearing. At least she was smart enough to have her feet covered. I was still in flip-flops.

"Y'all from 'round here? You don't look like you're as freezing cold as I am."

"No, we're from San Diego actually. Well, Houston before th—"

"Oh! Houston!" she said, keeping the "h" silent, so it came out, "Youston." "I just love it there, don't y'all? Dirk and I are from Texarkana. We're up here looking for some vacation property. Dirk just loves the mountains. Don't y'all just love the mountains?"

We both nodded. "Of course! We're actually out here on our honeymoon and—"

"Oh, y'all! Congratulations! How wonderful!" She bounced up and down, her boobs jiggling so much I was sure Michael was becoming hypnotized. "Now y'all are just out here trying to be alone and here we come bargin' in on your little love fest. I'll just go get us a seat inside and tell Dirk we need to leave y'all alone. We can sit by the fire inside and enjoy our cocoa.

"My name's Savannah, by the way. So sorry to interrupt y'all, but I do hope we'll see ya again real soon."

Savannah shook our hands quickly and sashayed back inside before we could get another word in, her strong perfume trailing behind her. Michael just shook his head at me and laughed. "My gosh, I felt like we were talking—or rather, listening to—my old college girlfriend. Big personality, big hair, and big mouth. Couldn't ever get a word in edgewise."

"I noticed you didn't mind her big boobs," I joked, looking back inside at Savannah.

"And I noticed you didn't mind Dirk's bulging biceps either," he sparred back, flexing his own arms to feel better about himself.

"You know I just love those biceps of yours, baby," I said, giving him my best Texas drawl and squeezing his big arms, which are just as nice and muscular, but not on display as Dirk's had been. "Now come on over here and give me some suga'." I gave him a big smooch and we both laughed, then continued to look at our menus, trying to decide what to eat.

After taking our time at dinner and sharing a scrumptious taco platter, we got some creamy, spiked hot cocoa to go and took a slow walk on the lighted path just around the resort property. The place was absolutely gorgeous. The fall foliage was just beginning to turn, and the yellow aspen leaves tinkled in the light breeze, lit up by the strategically placed lanterns. I could hear coyotes in the distance, and was thankful my cat, Daisy, wasn't around.

Before heading to our cabin, we stopped in the office to get information on trails nearby, as well as brochures from the resort spa. Hiking is hard on the feet and legs, if my twelve-year-old self remembered correctly. I wanted to make sure we made use of the massages and other amenities available to us as much as possible.

We finally reached our cabin, and as soon as the door opened, I felt the rush of warmth coming from the inside. Thank God they had turned on the heat. Laughing at my wimpy self shivering in the fifty-degree weather, I began to question my wardrobe selection for the week, wondering if I had packed enough layers. And then I looked up and stopped dead in my tracks. The place was amazing. While the cabin looked modest from the outside, the towering, fifteen-foot ceilings made it feel palatial on the inside. Large log beams accentuated the white walls, and the high-end but rustic furnishings gave the place a log-cabin-meets-farmhouse feel. I absolutely loved it. The natural wood burning fireplace was crackling, having been lit, I assumed, just recently by the invisible resort staff. A plush, white suede couch sat before it, and next to the couch, a distressed pedestal end table held a chilled bottle of champagne. I might have preferred Bailey's and more hot chocolate by that point instead, but I wasn't going to complain. I immediately felt at home.

Michael deposited our bags in the bedroom and I decided to quickly check my cell phone for any messages from Fritz. I had left it with the bags to enjoy a quiet dinner with my new hubby and to not appear as desperate for information as I really was.

Searching out our bags, I dug around in the outer pockets, feeling for my phone. Surprisingly, I came up empty-handed.

"Hon, have you seen my phone? I had put it in the outside pocket of my carry-on bag when I got out my jacket. But it's not here." I searched around inside the bag, certain I'd left it in the outside pocket, and continued to look around the room in vain. I hate it when I misplace that thing, but I do it more often than I'd like to admit.

"Maybe it fell out when the valet grabbed the bags. I'll call down and see if they've found it." Michael went to the room phone and called the front desk. He described my phone to them and the approximate time we arrived.

"They said they'll look around, but they haven't had a phone turned in yet. You sure you had it when we got here? You didn't leave it on the plane?"

"No. Remember? I checked it in the car. I know I had it when we got here. Maybe I dropped it outside."

"Did you try calling it?"

I took his advice and dialed my number from the room phone, but all I got was a click and my voice asking me to leave a message. Not helpful.

"I think it's dead. The battery was low on the trip up." I frowned.

"I'll go check the car real quick. You slip into something more comfortable and I'll be right back," Michael said. "I'm sure that's where it is." He took several long strides toward the door and sprinted outside. "I'll be back in two shakes!" he hollered back in a Southern drawl.

I grinned at my goofy husband's antics and kept looking. Maybe I'd put it in a pocket of another bag, or maybe it had fallen out and the valet stuck it somewhere else. I was increasingly desperate to check my phone, and with Michael gone for a few minutes, I could do so with less guilt.

Twenty minutes later, I had not found my phone, and neither had Michael. The front desk called to say they hadn't found anything outside, but they'd keep looking in the morning.

"It's no big deal, babe," Michael assured me. "It must have fallen out somewhere. I know you're antsy to check it, so we'll just go into town tomorrow and get you a new phone if it's not been found. We can call your carrier and transfer your line over. It will be like it was never gone at all."

I sighed and agreed as Michael pulled me in toward him. Maybe this was a sign that I should stop worrying about what might be and just focus on my sweet husband and our awesome honeymoon in this luxurious place. *Everything will work out,* I kept telling myself, not too convincingly. Michael began to slowly massage my back and shoulders, his breath warm on my neck. I could feel the tension that had again built up slowly begin to fade.

"You know we have our own hot tub in this place, right?" he whispered in my ear, his strong hands kneading my muscles with ease. "I think you need to relax, and lucky for you," he laughed softly in his deep, sexy voice, "I know exactly what you need..."

• CHAPTER 8 •

MONDAY MORNING CAME and Michael and I were happily awakened by a phone call from the front desk, saying someone had turned in my phone. Thank God! I hastily threw my hair into a ponytail, brushed my teeth, threw on some sweats, and made my way to the office. The morning air was brisk, but despite the cold, I could feel myself begin to sweat in anticipation. I was anxious to know if I would have any information from Fritz.

"Good morning, Mrs. Drake," said the lady at the front desk. The young woman was about my height, with beautiful long, dark, wavy hair. Probably in her twenties, she had dark brown eyes, and a gorgeous tan complexion with nary a blemish or wrinkle. Her nametag said, "Caty", but how did she know who I was? Probably because I was the only person with bed head standing there, tapping my hands on the counter, out of breath, and looking like I needed a cell phone fix. I had sheet impressions on my face and puffy eyes. She was lucky I had clothes on.

"Hi, do you have my cell phone?" I asked quickly. Why bother with polite chatter? It was seven in the morning, I would normally still be sleeping, and I wanted my phone...badly.

"Can you verify any identifying markers on it? You know, prove that it's yours somehow?"

My jaw dropped.

"I'm kidding, hon. Shouldn't tease you about that, maybe. I know I'd be lost without mine." Caty gave me a smile and handed me my phone.

"Be sure to head on down to the restaurant for breakfast anytime. This morning's special is espresso waffles with mocha drizzle, served with a side of sausage and cinnamon apples."

She had me at espresso. But really, I was more interested in my phone. I'd think about breakfast in a minute.

"You are an angel, Caty. Thank you, thank you, thank you!" I quickly keyed in my password as I turned around to head back, only to get an error that the battery was low and it was shutting itself down. Fabulous. I hurried back to the cabin so it could charge. Would I have a message from Fritz? I was desperate to know.

"Hey, you're back," Michael said as he rolled over in bed when I walked into the bedroom. He sat up, stretched, and beckoned me closer. "You jumped out of bed way too early this morning."

"I know, but they found my phone!" I sat down on the bed next to him, unplugged his phone from the charger, and replaced it with mine.

"Oh, really? Someone turned it in?" He yawned and I marveled at how good guys look in the morning when they just wake up. They look all cute and warm and fuzzy. Why is that? Why doesn't he have bags under his eyes, facial blemishes, and totally freaked out hair?

"Remember the phone call we got about fifteen minutes ago?"

"Mmmm, not really. You wore me out last night," he said, grabbing me in a bear hug. Men may look good in the morning, but they still have morning breath like the rest of us. I slowly disentangled from him, trying not to inhale.

"I should rinse out my mouth is what you're saying?" he grinned. "Be right back. Then you can tell me what happened."

"Actually, I don't know. I didn't ask." Michael went into the bathroom to brush his teeth while I continued. "I was so happy to have it back that I just grabbed it and ran back up here to plug it in. It's deader than dead." I checked the phone once to be sure, but it was at about 3% battery after that whopping two minutes of charge time. No luck. I continued to stare at it, pleading with it silently to charge faster.

Michael walked back into the room. "Well, while it charges, why don't we go get some breakfast? Take your mind off of it for a bit, and let the thing actually get some juice." He eyed my bouncing leg.

"Okay," I sighed, knowing he was right. "That's a good idea. And I am starving." I jumped up off the bed and walked into the bathroom to put just a tad bit of makeup on. I gasped when I saw myself in the mirror. My hair was matted on one side of my head, I had giant bags under my eyes, and a tiny bit of drool had crusted on my chin. How had I let myself go out looking like this?! Michael put on some clothes, ran his fingers through his hair, and was ready to go, of course. I had to spend ten minutes making myself look presentable. Life is unfair. We grabbed our room key and headed out the door.

Less than an hour later, we were back in our cabin, jacked up on espresso waffles, maple syrup, and coffee. Thankfully, my phone was charged enough to check messages. I had a text from Fritz. *Call me.* My heart immediately began to race.

I was supposed to be getting my stuff ready to go out on a hike, but instead I slipped out onto the back patio with my phone while Michael filled our CamelBaks in the kitchenette. The patio area was cozy but impressive. A large firepit stood in the middle with cushioned sectional furniture surrounding it. Trees and shrubs on either end ensured privacy while still allowing for a magnificent view of the valley below. While it was still freezing outside, I hardly felt it.

My hands shook, and I silently dialed Fritz and held my breath. I paced back and forth across the patio, barely noticing the view. One ring. Two rings. Three rings. Pick up the damn phone, already!

"Mmmm, hello?" a sleepy voice answered.

"Fritz?" I squeaked out, stopping in my tracks. "You said to call. What did you find?" I quickly glanced inside. Still no Michael.

"Good God, woman, what time is it?" He yawned loudly in my ear, and I could hear his whiskers scraping the phone as he stretched.

"It's, uh," I checked my watch, "9:30 your time. Why are you still asleep? What did you need to tell me?" *Come on, come on,* I silently pleaded.

"Hold your horses! Geez. Let a man get his bearings." He sat there for a minute, breathing in my ear. I could just imagine his white hair sticking out all willy nilly. Fritz is one of the few men I can think of that looks as good as I do in the mornings. "Okay, I think I'm awake now." He sighed deeply. "I was up most of the night following leads on your dad. He's a tough nut to crack, let me tell ya. Damn government databases and their security measures." I heard him rifling through some papers. Man, I hoped he hadn't gone into his "office" in the bathroom.

"What do you mean 'government databases?' What did you find?" Spill it, for goodness' sake!

"Well, this would have been a lot easier if you had told me your dad had an WAUHAAYYEEHHBAAAHHAHH." More yawning. I held the phone away from my ear.

"That he had a what?"

"An FBI file. He's listed as a person of interest."

I sat there for a beat, silent.

"My dad wasn't wanted by the FBI." I stood there for a minute and could feel my blood pressure rise. My frustration was mounting. Was this some kind of joke? "Have you been talking to Lisa? The last thing I want right now is to be teased about my dad being a secret agent or having anything to do with the FBI. Come on, Fritz, I'm on my honeym—"

"Emily, hold up." He paused and his tone got very serious. "I would not have called you on your honeymoon if I hadn't found something. Right?"

I exhaled slowly and nodded, though obviously he couldn't see me. He wouldn't call me as a joke, or even on just a hunch. I knew that. Fritz is very good at what he does, and he takes it very seriously. I started getting dizzy, thinking of the significance of his words, and forced myself to relax.

"George Potens, AKA your dad, was on the FBI's radar, kid."

"*Was*? What? Why?" I asked with a pleading voice. I could not believe this was true. My dad had been as clean as the day is long. Thoughts cluttered my brain. Even if my dad *had been* an FBI person of interest, surely there was an explanation. But right now, my focus remained on knowing whether he was still alive. I needed to know!

But still, he had an FBI file. The implications of this news rocked me. Did this mean my dad had been involved in criminal activity? Why else would he be on the FBI's radar? I couldn't believe I was even thinking that. But, if so, was he in hiding? Did he really die in that car accident, or was he alive? Would I ever find out the truth?

"Was...is...who knows?" Fritz continued, oblivious to the thoughts running through my head. "That's still TBD. The FBI file lists him as 'Presumed Dead.' I haven't gotten ahold of Father, but I left a message at the place he's staying when he arrives, and I did let them know it's urgent.

"Listen, kid, the feds have a big ass file on your dad, and most of it is redacted. Even I can't get past that. Well, yet anyway. I'm still working on it. But, Emily," he sighed, and I could hear him scratching his face, "there's a shit-ton of intel about him here. And I have a feeling I've only just scratched the surface."

• CHAPTER 9 •

I HUNG UP WITH FRITZ and stood in a daze for what was probably only seconds, but it felt like hours. I dropped my head and closed my eyes. It was as if I had never known my father at all. The happy-go-lucky, loving, and reliable man I had grown up with was a person of interest with the FBI. Why? It made no sense. I thought back to all of the big business transactions I had known about. None stood out as dangerous or illegal. I never recalled my mom voicing any concerns about business partners or scandalous deals. I certainly hadn't known the ins and outs of my dad's days, but I'd never questioned him. Why would I?

Slowly, I walked inside to tell Michael what Fritz had found. Together we stood in the kitchenette, dumbfounded. He was as confused as I was. We were still no closer to finding the person who left the note at the wedding. But knowing that the FBI had been watching my dad...well, it nearly drove me out of my mind. What had he been up to? What on earth was he involved in that garnered him a "big ass", mostly redacted file? It drove me crazy with worry. If he were alive now, and if he knew all along that he'd been on the FBI's radar, what were the chances of me ever seeing him again?

I mentally kicked myself for not going over the files from his home office more carefully when he'd, well, *supposedly* maybe, died. Instead, everything related to his business dealings had been boxed up and given to the lawyers that handled the estate. As a kid, I had never been too familiar with that part of his life. And as an adult, why would I question him? To me, he was just an entrepreneur who dealt in profitable real estate deals. He had an office at home. It's not like he kept it behind locked doors. I mean, some of his drawers and cabinets were locked, but I could go in whenever I wanted to. The real estate deals—or what I thought were real estate deals—required occasional travel, but it's not like he disappeared for months at a time and altered his appearance. He didn't live looking over his shoulder, waiting for trouble. He always made good money and we never wanted for anything, and I guess I just never questioned it. Had his property acquisitions, like the one he'd worked on in Louisiana prior to his apparent death, just been a hobby? Or simply a cover? Did he have a nefarious side to him? Had my mom known? Or had she been in the dark too? What exactly was he involved in? All the questions made my head spin.

I was in a fog and grew increasingly irritated and confused. There was a good chance my dad had been involved in some kind of criminal activity for who knows how long. Had one of his deals led to their deaths? Was he even really dead?

I walked to the couch and sat down, putting my head in my hands. Michael sat down next to me, wrapping his arms around me.

"Babe," he said, tucking my hair behind my ear, "I don't know what to say. Frankly, I'm just blown away by this, and a little freaked out." He laughed quietly. "Sounds like your dad was, or is, a little scarier than I ever imagined." He rubbed my shoulders with his strong hands, kneading out the knots that had again begun to form. "I'm sorry you've been kept in the dark about this, but your dad must've had a good reason. You don't *know* that your dad was doing anything criminal. An FBI watch list just means they're keeping an eye out for him." I rolled my head back and forth as he worked out the kinks in my neck. "Maybe he was dealing with some bad guys unknowingly. You certainly found that out in Louisiana. I'm sure he was completely innocent of any wrongdoing."

"You're not on an FBI watch list if you're completely innocent of any wrongdoing," I said, stone-faced. "My dad must have had some secrets that he kept from us. But why?"

Michael sighed loudly, and I looked up to see his brow creased in concern, a slight look of guilt on his face.

"What? Is there something *you* need to tell me?" I asked, startled. Was Michael hiding something from me? He waited a beat without saying anything, and I could sense his discomfort.

"Omigod, Michael. If you are about to tell me you're on some kind of watch list, or you've lied to me, or kept secrets from me, I promise you I will lose it!" I couldn't take any more bizarre revelations. This...well, this had been enough. More than enough.

"No, no, nothing like that. I've always said I wouldn't lie to you, and I haven't. But I did leave something out. A lie of omission, I guess, not really a secret. I thought it was for the best."

I waited a minute, fifty thousand possibilities running through my head. Michael shifted around uncomfortably, delaying the inevitable.

"Apparently our house was broken into during our wedding. Maria and Candy called to tell me about it that night after they got back to the house and saw the door busted open. That's who called my cell right after we got to the cottage and scared the shit out of us." He laughed quietly at the memory. I didn't. My head shot up and I searched his face. I couldn't believe he'd kept this from me.

"Daisy?" I asked frantically, the safety of my sweet kitty being the first thing that came to mind. "Is she all right?"

"Yes, she's fine. And, oddly enough nothing appears to have been taken." He shook his head. "But the place was trashed." He turned and looked at me, rubbing my arms gently. "I'm sure it was a case of mistaken identity. We've only owned it for a few weeks. Most likely whoever broke in thought they were still dealing with the former owner. Maybe looking for drugs or something."

We'd bought a bit of a fixer-upper, knowing Michael could easily do the work, and most of our stuff was still in storage and boxes. The house looked a little rough from the outside (and inside), but I never assumed the former owners were into anything bad. Thank God no one was there besides Daisy.

I felt numb. What else could happen this week? I stared at Michael, unable to form words. I couldn't believe that it had happened on our wedding night.

"I didn't tell you because I didn't want you to worry. The girls took care of it, called the police, changed the locks. Everyone's fine. Nothing is missing. And I told the girls not to dare bother you about it.

"We're on our honeymoon. And the whole thing with your dad...well, the last thing I wanted to do was give you something else to worry about. I felt it was taken care of properly, and there was nothing else we could do. I'm sorry I didn't tell you right away. I really am."

Oddly enough, with everything else that was going on, I felt I was becoming immune to shocking news. Knowing our house was broken into would have sent me into a panic a few weeks ago, but now, so separated from the incident both literally and figuratively, my anxiety abated quickly, and soon I hardly felt anything but concern for the girls.

"Do Maria and Candy feel okay staying there after all of this?" I asked. "I don't want them to feel unsafe. They're doing us a huge favor."

"Yeah, I talked with them about that. They're totally fine with it. Apparently, some hot cop showed up when they called 9-1-1 and Maria got his number. He's promised to do extra surveillance in the neighborhood and they're going on a double-date with him and his buddy tonight. I, uh, think it's all working out for the best." He smiled. "You okay?" he asked, looking at me with concern. "This has been one helluva honeymoon so far, hasn't it?"

I dropped my hands into my lap and turned to gaze into his eyes. This man was my husband. This gorgeous, loving man was here to help me through this. For the first time in a long time, I didn't have to go at it alone. And I was so thankful for that. I willed myself to relax.

"Well, not all of it's been bad," I told him. I exhaled deeply and gave him a sly smile. I shook my head, trying to free myself of my worries and concerns—if only temporarily. Then I gently pushed him back onto the couch and kissed him until I forgot about everything else from the past few days—the note from my dad, the FBI, the burglary. Right then and there, I only allowed one thing to be on my mind.

Later on, Michael and I got in a short, five-mile roundtrip hike up to a beautiful mountain lake where we ate a delicious lunch the resort had packed for us. We stretched out on the rocks in the sun, stared at the clear skies, and relaxed, basking in the beauty of the Rockies. We nibbled on delicious ham sandwiches, cucumber salad, and amazingly thick and gooey chocolate chip cookies the size of my hand. The exercise cleared my head, and I did my best to ignore the nagging thoughts that kept coming into my brain.

On the trail up, we had encountered several other hikers from various parts of the country, even some students from Japan, and enjoyed our brief encounters with them. Everyone's always happy on a gorgeous mountain hike. Funnily enough, more than halfway back down the trail, we ran into Dirk and Savannah, just making their way up.

"Omigod, y'all, how much farther?" Savannah asked breathlessly. "I swear we've been walkin' for hours." Her Christian Louboutin boots probably weren't the best for hiking, and she'd stripped down to a tight tank top and shorts, only to start shivering once she stopped moving. "And now I gotta pee. Is there a bathroom 'round here?"

Dirk was loaded up with all of their gear, his backpack bursting at the seams, Savannah's shed clothes peeking out of every nook and cranny. He carried a large and heavy camera on a strap around his neck. Sweat dripped from his dark hairline down his cheeks.

Once Savannah realized the closest bathroom was behind the nearest tree, she decided she didn't need to go so badly anymore, and they kept moving. Michael did warn them that if they went all the way to the top, it might be dark by the time they made it back down. Trying to find your way down a mountain trail at night in the dark can be very hard. It's easy to lose the path, temperatures plummet after dark, and animals come out looking for prey. I sure hoped they would heed his advice and turn around sooner rather than later. Of course, if they were stuck and needed to start a fire, they could always cut off some of Savannah's hair to use as kindling. Her whole head was extremely flammable. I snickered at the thought. Man, I am a bad person. I am a bad, bad person.

As we continued down the mountain, we made our way across a ridge with an incredible view of the landscape. The beauty of it compelled us to stop for a bit to take it all in. Too often I find myself hiking to a destination, my eyes set on the ground. Out here in this gorgeous landscape, I wanted to make an effort to enjoy my amazing surroundings. The mountains seemed to reach to the heavens, pine trees and golden aspen dotted the hillsides, and the peaks, barren of vegetation, were already covered in snow. A panoramic view of some of the tallest mountains in the region made for a fantastic spot for pictures and selfies.

After drinking some water, we put our phones away and decided to keep moving. I noticed clouds beginning to roll in, and a slight chill was unexpectedly in the air. As the wind began to pick up, we again started our trek down the mountain, only to stop soon thereafter when our phones started beeping.

"Must have cell service right here in this spot," Michael commented. I grabbed the phone from my pocket and a text from Fritz popped up on my screen.

Got ahold of Father. Call me.

"Omigod, Michael!" I stammered as I read him the text, and my heart pounded against my chest. What had Fritz found out? Was my dad really alive? Or was someone playing a cruel joke on me?

"He sent me the same thing," Michael said, looking at his own phone. I immediately dialed Fritz, but my phone beeped again. My heart sank. No signal. We looked at each other for an instant, our eyes locking, a silent understanding passing between us. We'd have service in the trailhead parking lot, most likely. But probably not again before then. We nodded, thinking the same thing. "Let's go!" Turning on our heels, we both dashed down the trail as if our lives depended on it.

Reaching the parking lot in what had to be record time, I doubled over to catch my breath. "Call Fritz!" I squeaked out to Michael, who wasn't having nearly the trouble breathing that I was.

"Calling," Michael said as he sprayed his head down with his water bottle before taking a drink. He looked at his phone quizzically and held it up high, walking circles in the small parking lot. Only two vehicles were left: ours, and a black truck that must have belonged to Dirk and Savannah. Most people were finished hiking and had left the trails this late in the day. "Damn!" Michael grunted, wiping his face. "No signal here either."

"What?" I looked down at my phone. Sure enough. No bars. Lifting my gaze to the sky, I saw dark, gray clouds rolling in. We'd probably get a signal a few miles down the road in town, but not right here with a storm coming. Thankful we were off the trail, I began to wonder about Dirk and Savannah still out there as the wind began to blow even harder.

"Let's roll into town and get something warm to drink," Michael suggested. "The temp is dropping fast out here. I'm sure we'll have cell service in town."

"I'm kinda worried, babe." I looked up at the mountain that no longer looked quiet and peaceful with a storm rolling in. Instead, it looked dark and ominous, and I felt a strange sense of foreboding. "Dirk and Savannah are still on the trail. Do you think they'll be okay?" Thunder rumbled in the distance, spurring us to head to the SUV and put our backpacks inside.

"Well, Dirk's backpack was big enough to house a small village. I know that much." Michael paused and guzzled some more water. "Surely, they have some rain gear in there, and they know enough to stay away from tall trees in the lightning."

"I sure hope so," I conceded. We hopped inside the SUV just as raindrops started to fall. Big, fat drops splattered heavily on the windshield, and before we knew it, it was a full-on deluge.

"Let's get to town," Michael said, pulling out of the parking lot as the dirt roads quickly turned to mud. I turned back and thought about Dirk and Savannah still on the trail. Had they found shelter? Would they be okay? Would Savannah's helmet hair even be affected by the rain? I caught a flash of color amid the trees but realized it could not have been them. There's no way they had come down the trail as quickly as we had. They were still up there, on the mountain, exposed. I prayed that the storm would quickly pass through and they'd safely find their way back down before dark.

• CHAPTER 10 •

ONCE IN TOWN, WE FOUND OUR WAY to a local coffee shop and ordered some hot drinks. I got out my phone with trembling hands, temporarily forgetting about Dirk and Savannah, and frantically dialed Fritz's number. I walked to the back of the shop, struggling to calm myself down. A knot formed in my stomach at the thought of what new information he might have to share.

"Yeah, Emily, I got some news," he said as his greeting.

"What?! WHAT?!" I practically screamed. The man next to me glanced up, eyed me warily, and slowly took a few steps away.

"Is Michael with you?"

"Yes, of course he is." I looked around the shop, the rain still pounding on the metal roof, and spotted Michael picking up our drinks from the barista.

"Well, kid, I'm afraid it's not good news."

My face fell. I could feel tears begin to well up in my eyes. I wanted to hang up right then and there.

"I talked to Father." Fritz paused, and the words I didn't want to hear came out. "The man he saw at the wedding was not your dad."

I stood silent for a beat. "How do you know for sure?" I asked defiantly, rubbing my eyes. "Father had never even met my dad before the wedding." I struggled to come up with reasons he might not be recognized. Maybe he'd been scarred from the accident or had plastic surgery since then.

"Well, for one, he was young. Father guessed mid-thirties." Damn. Even a plastic surgeon couldn't erase twenty-plus years. "Dark, wavy hair, a few tats." He took a deep breath and exhaled. "This guy was certainly not your dad. And unless you have a long-lost twin brother, I'm guessing he wasn't even a family member."

"No, no twin brother." I sighed miserably and paused for a minute to compose myself. "What's this guy's end game? I don't get it. Why would some random person leave me a note supposedly from my dad?"

"Hell, maybe it is from your dad. Maybe he had someone else leave the note for him."

"Maybe," I said, not convinced. I felt completely deflated. Michael walked up with a look of concern on his face, and we leaned against the bar beside us. My heart was hurting. I had been convinced my dad had left that note. Now I was doubtful just like the rest of them.

Fritz continued. "I'm not giving up hope yet, kid. And just for shits and grins, I took that paper pulp you globbed on me at the reception and got it to a lab in Houston for testing. Personally, I think it's not going to yield anything, but you never know.

"I'll keep looking into his FBI file and let you know if I get any further with it. And I'll call you if I find out anything about the paper. See if, by some miracle, I can get a handwriting sample off it or something. Keep your chin up. We'll figure out who's behind this."

Fritz and I hung up and, once again, I filled Michael in on our conversation. He just shook his head, probably wondering in the back of his mind just what the hell he had gotten into by marrying me. Dad with an FBI file. Strangers leaving me notes at our wedding. We walked outside to the covered porch that backed up to the Big Thompson River and sat our drinks down before collapsing in the chairs. I undid my boot laces and slid my socked feet out, propping them up on Michael's lap.

"I'm sorry, babe," he said, massaging my feet gently. "But at least now you have an answer. Not the answer you wanted, though."

I looked out at the water rushing by, the roaring sound strangely comforting. That note had been a glimmer of hope, now dashed by the fact that it wasn't delivered by my dad at all, but some stranger. I guess his handwriting could have been forged by anyone, chicken scratch that it was. I was naïve to think it was from him. He and my mom had died in a car accident. And him having an FBI file didn't change that fact. I needed to get my head on straight and quit thinking like the dramas I watch on TV. No one would be coming back from the dead. No more deep, dark secrets would be revealed. I needed to focus on my future and be thankful for what I had right here in front of me.

I slowly got up, peeled off my socks, and walked down to the edge of the water. The rain was now just a sprinkle. Carefully, I stepped in, the icy cold temperature shocking my feet and legs. Michael slowly came up behind me and wrapped me in an embrace, holding me steady as I let the water wash away all of the aches and pains of my body, and of my heart.

Later that evening, I was so bushed from the emotional rollercoaster of the day that we decided to order room service and enjoy a nice dinner out on our patio. Michael even ordered the fixings for s'mores, grabbed some logs, and lit the outdoor fireplace. We brought out blankets from inside and snuggled under them, toasting our marshmallows and feeding each other the gooey treats. It was a beautiful fall night. Elk called to each other in the valley below, and owls hooted from far away. The fire crackled and I laid my head on Michael's shoulder.

"What should we do tomorrow?" I asked, willing to get all thoughts of what might have been out of my mind. "Do you have anything in mind?" I was so mentally exhausted, I didn't want to make one more decision. Spending all day at the spa would have suited me just fine.

"How about a longer hike followed by a deep tissue massage? I need to work these kinks out." Michael stretched his arms overhead and cracked his neck. As a professional contractor, he does physical work every day. My physical work entails running on the beach followed by some yoga stretches. Well, I also move antiques around at the shop, but that doesn't compare to his daily load of physicality.

"That sounds great." I silently made a pact with myself to quit worrying and just enjoy the rest of our time here. So far, our honeymoon had been repeatedly marred by events related to me. I was tired of all that and just wanted to focus on both of us enjoying our newly wedded bliss. A nice hike followed by a massage would be just what the doctor ordered. I smiled and sighed, licking the last of the marshmallow off my fingers.

"I'm going to go inside to wash my hands and grab some water. You want anything?"

Michael shook his head no. I stood up and walked back inside to grab a drink. Coming back out, I glanced up at the television he had left on, volume down low. He had been occasionally checking for updates on his favorite NFL team playing Monday Night Football. A commercial break came on with a local news report, and I hesitated at the door.

The headline, "Gas Leak Leads to Small Explosion in Business District," scrolled across the screen. I paused, watching what had to be amateur video, showing very shaky footage of a family smiling in the foreground, just before an explosion rocked the building behind them.

"Tourists get video of an explosion that occurred today at an abandoned building in the heart of the business district," the off-screen reporter said. "The building, owned by C-IZZY, Inc, of Matamoras, Mexico, is considered a total loss. No injuries have been reported..."

Wow, I thought. *That's so close to where we were today. Thank God no one was hurt.* I continued to look at the screen, watching screaming people fleeing the scene as mayhem ensued.

"...but authorities continue to look into just how a gas leak at the building could have occurred. Stay tuned to KVKX for more details."

The video went to freeze-frame just before cutting out. It caught the panic of the moment, children crying, parents sheltering kids, and a running bystander, face determined, jaw set...and very much my dad.

• CHAPTER 11 •

MY GLASS SHATTERED AS IT HIT THE FLOOR, narrowly missing my feet. Michael shot up and propelled himself over the bench in one swift move, at my side in an instant.

"What's going on? You okay?" He looked around at the shards of glass at my feet. "Don't move. I'll get this cleaned up." I couldn't move, but he didn't know the true reason. My eyes were glued to the screen even though the football game had resumed. I had seen my dad. My dad was alive. He was *here in Elkston. Today*!

"You didn't get cut, did you?" Michael asked, finally looking up at my face. "Emily?" Taking hold my arms, he shook me gently. "Emily, what happened?" He looked up at the TV, now back on the game. "You that excited that the Texans are winning?"

I finally shook myself out of my stupor and began to stammer, pointing at the screen.

"What? Your dad liked the Texans too? Is that so shocking?" He grinned and carefully continued to pick up the broken pieces of glass.

"No." I stopped and took a deep breath, willing my heart to slow down. "My dad was on TV," I squeaked, but it only came out as a whisper. I felt like I was in a dream, trying to shout out and not making any noise at all. I grabbed Michael's arm and stopped him, looked him in the eye and forced myself to settle down, finding my voice. "My dad was on TV. I saw him." I explained to Michael the news story and exactly what I had seen.

"Wait." He paused, shaking his head. "You're saying your dad is alive? And he was here? In Elkston?" He stared past me, taking it all in, a slight look of doubt in his eyes. "You are 100% positive the man you saw on TV was your dad?" I nodded. "I mean, you've had some weird news the past few days. Do you think your mind is playing tricks on you?"

"No, Michael. I'm absolutely sure it was him." And I was. I knew it. No doubt in my mind. That was him. I stood there, still in shock, my breathing shallow as a thousand thoughts raced through my mind. I needed Michael to believe me. I was not seeing things. I had seen my dad.

Michael let out a deep sigh as he deposited the remaining chunks of glass in the trash. "Wow. Okay. First, FBI, and now, uh, this," he muttered, rubbing the back of his neck. He grabbed a wet towel and wiped up all the remaining tiny shards of glass before taking my hand. He looked me in the eyes. I knew he was determined to believe me, no matter how crazy I sounded. "Well, this honeymoon is about to get a lot more interesting. Call Fritz," he said, nodding his head. "Get him down here now."

I ran to get my phone and immediately called Fritz, breathlessly filling him in on all of the details.

"Hot damn, woman! You sure know how to ratchet things up." Fritz chuckled and I could hear the anticipation in his voice. "I'll be there as soon as I can. Get the video footage from the station and we'll start with that." I could hear him moving around, already making preparations. "Shit, where's my duffel? Ah, hell, I can't find anything in this mess."

Fritz had his office in his home, and his wife, Zoey, helped out with cases and also kept conditions livable. "What, is Zoey out of town for a few days?"

"What? Oh, Zoey's gone. Went to stay with her sister for a few weeks. Said she needed a break from me. It happens." I chuckled to myself. Fritz can be a handful. He and Zoey have been married a long time, probably only because she gives herself permission to leave every once in a while. "Ah, here it is. As I was saying, get the video footage, but you need to keep a low profile in town. Your dad must be hiding for a reason, and if he gets a glimpse of you, he might just take off. You stay put at your fancy pants luxury resort and let me handle this."

"Where will you stay?"

"I don't know, but I'll find something."

Fritz called the airlines, but all flights into Denver from Dallas were booked, so he worked a deal with a buddy to get a flight into an airstrip normally reserved for the rich and famous. I know it pained him to do that, socialist that he is. We arranged for Michael to pick him up in the morning.

I put in a call to the TV station that same night, and surprisingly, someone picked up. I explained the situation, skipping most of the facts and adding my own embellishments, but was told the reporter who worked the story was also the morning news anchor; thus, she was not available and probably already asleep. They refused to give me her cell number, but said they'd give her my message. I was at a dead end until morning.

The whole night I lay there, my mind racing. My dad was alive! Was my mom too? Had their accident in the Louisiana swamp been a setup? What had really happened? How could he have let them be declared dead and stay hidden all that time? It had to be related to the FBI file, didn't it? Otherwise it made no sense. My bitterness was increasing by the second. Who fakes his own death and breaks his only child's heart? But maybe he had a good reason. Were they in witness protection? I lay there, conflicted, for hours. Michael slept peacefully next to me, an occasional snort escaping his lips. Eventually, I drifted off and dreamed of alligators crawling into our bed, pulling me and Michael into the swamp, while my parents stood at the door, watching and laughing.

• CHAPTER 12 •

I WAS UP BEFORE THE SUN, lying in bed with Michael's arm thrown across my belly. I ran my fingers along the outline of his muscles and snuggled closer to him. He was my only refuge in the craziness my life had, once again, become. As I laid there counting my blessings, he wrapped his arm around me and slowly began to wake up, nuzzling my neck. I rolled over to face him and he pulled me flush against his warm body, fully awake now with one thing on his mind, his strong hands caressing me gently. Closing my mind off to all my worries, I let myself get lost in him, letting his strength, passion, and love fuel me.

Afterward, I cupped his face with my hand, tracing the lines of his jaw, my thumb brushing over his lips. I looked into his deep, blue eyes.

"I love you," I said. "I love you so much. I'm sorry my life is such a mess right now, and I'm sorry I'm ruining our honeymoon."

"You're not ruining anything, babe," he said, grabbing my hand and kissing my fingertips, one by one. "I wouldn't rather be anyplace else or with anyone else or...doing anything else," he said, wiggling his eyebrows. "We'll get through this.

"I do have to admit though, I am a little afraid of my now-alive, possible fugitive father-in-law, but I'll get over that." He grinned. I let out a small laugh at the thought of my six-foot-two-inch, built-like-Adonis husband being afraid of anyone, let alone my dad, the world's most amicable guy. Tears came to my eyes as memories of my dad flooded my brain. Did I really even know him? Now I wasn't so sure.

"Hey," Michael said, gently wiping the tears from my face, "it's going to be okay. I promise. We're going to find your dad, get everything figured out, and go back to California to have and raise our eight kids." I laughed and punched him lightly in the chest. He rose from the bed and walked into the bathroom. I admired my husband's sexy physique as I watched him go, and I couldn't help but smile. I heard him turn the shower water on, and a few seconds later, his head popped out.

"Come on," he said, beckoning me. "I'll rub your back in the shower. And, who knows...maybe do other things too." He grinned and raised the one eyebrow, teasing me. I willingly obliged.

When we got out of the shower, I checked my cell phone, praying the news reporter had tried to get ahold of me. Not surprisingly, she hadn't. I sat down on our bed and willed myself to be patient. She probably just got off the air and was...what? Taking a nap? I would be if I got up at 3:00 a.m. to work. I looked around the room to find anything else to keep my mind occupied. Michael had run down to grab some breakfast, but I couldn't even think about eating. I had to get ahold of that reporter. I grabbed a book to read but tossed it aside. My patience lasted a whole thirty seconds, and I placed a call to the station. Miraculously, she answered.

"KVKX, Darcy Jensen," she said quickly.

"Oh, hi. Um, my name's Emily Potens, I mean, Drake, and I, um, I need your help." Ugh. This woman wouldn't take me seriously at all talking like that. I hadn't been expecting her to answer the station's phone and hadn't prepared what I was going to say. What was I thinking?! She sighed loudly. "I'm sorry," I explained, trying to start over. "I didn't know *you* would actually answer the phone, but you are the one I want to talk to."

"Well, at this Podunk station, we only have so many on staff. I'm morning news anchor, afternoon reporter, receptionist when I'm in the office, and gopher when I'm not. What have you got?"

I explained to her that I saw a person in the video of yesterday's story I hadn't been able to locate for almost two years.

"So call the police," she said abruptly, sounding bored and annoyed. "Is this a missing person's case?"

"Not really," I told her, "he's been declared dead." Crap! Mental face palm. Probably shouldn't have told her that.

"Hmmm, now this is getting interesting. You saw a guy that's been presumed dead running past the scene of an unexplained explosion in the downtown business district of a tourist town. Is he Middle Eastern? Maybe on the FBI's Most Wanted?" Her tone completely changed, and I could hear her practically salivating. The thought hadn't even crossed my mind that my dad could somehow be connected to the explosion. I was too stunned just knowing he was alive.

"Omigod, no!" I exclaimed. "He's my dad. And he's not Middle Eastern. Not that only Middle Easterners blow up buildings. But geez, he's not on the FBI's Most Wanted! Only a person of interest!" Omigod, my brain! Did I really tell that to a *reporter*?!

"Please," I continued, "I just need a copy of the footage. That's all. And the approximate time of day would be helpful. Just those things. I promise I won't bother you anymore."

"And all I need is a good story to break me out of this godforsaken small-town market. And this might be it. Listen," she continued, "I'll get you your footage. But I want in."

"I can't let you *in*. There's nothing to be *in* on."

"Like hell there's not. You've got an FBI POI who's played dead for two years—"

"Eighteen months, really," I cut in.

"Fine. He's played dead for eighteen months, and now he's caught on camera running from the scene of a building explosion. And not just any building, but a building that's a hotbed for drug activity."

"What?" What was she saying? I had no idea what she was talking about. I knew that pot shops were flying up all over the place in this state, but that's legal. How exactly was this building a hotbed for drug activity? I thought it was abandoned?

"Yeah. I've heard some things," she continued. "The building's been under the local PD's watch lately. They suspect it's being used as a warehouse and distribution center for narcotics. But knowing these small townies who are soooo in love with their tourists, now that the building's gone, they'll probably drop any investigation into it. Wouldn't make for good press."

"Well, that's too bad, but how does that relate to me? My dad wasn't involved in the explosion."

"And how do you know that, exactly? You said you haven't seen him in almost two years!"

She had a point. Dammit. What the hell *was* my dad involved in?

"I just need the footage," I pleaded.

"And I just need a story!" Her tone shifted. "Emily Potens-Drake, or whatever your name is, I think we can help each other out. How about we set up a meet?"

A *meet?* This sounded so sketchy. My mind reeled. How had my honeymoon, much less my life, come to this? Was my dad running from the scene of a crime? That thought almost made me laugh. My dad was the most clean-cut, straight-laced person I had ever known. But with everything else that had come out, what did I know? What should I do? Could I trust this woman? Fritz had told me not to go into town for fear of being spotted. Plus, Michael had to pick up Fritz, so I wouldn't have a car. Did the remote Rockies have Uber? I sat for a bit and stewed. Finally, I decided on my plan of action. I took a deep breath and exhaled slowly.

"Fine, we can meet. But you have to come here."

"You bet," she said. "Name the place and time." Well, that was easy. I told her where we were staying and the easiest route to get there. "Swanky!" she exclaimed. "I'll gladly come there. Think you can get me some spa services? I could really use a pedi." Did she really just ask for a pedi? Man, she was pushing it.

"How about we go on a hike?" I countered. "There are some trails out here, and we can talk in private." I really didn't want to invite her into our cabin yet. That seemed too intrusive. This was our sanctuary, and I didn't want some stranger invading it with her notebook and her questions.

"How about we *don't*. I don't even own a pair of hiking boots, and my tennis shoes are meant to be worn only under the supervision of a personal trainer in the gym."

I had visions of a twenty-something diva in three-inch heels with caked-on makeup and a Botoxed face.

"Okay, we'll have some lunch at the restaurant."

"I'm vegan and I only have a sixteen-ounce, wheatgrass smoothie for lunch." She really wasn't leaving me with many options.

"Fine," I sighed. "I'll call the spa."

I set up two pedicures for me and Darcy later that morning. I didn't figure we should go get a couples massage, and she flat out told me no sauna time since she'd just gotten her spray tan. She seemed a little high maintenance to me.

Darcy arrived a little while later and drove straight to the cabin in her compact SUV. Upon initial inspection, I found her to be a typical TV personality; loads of makeup, bright red lipstick, deep brown, perfectly styled hair that cascaded down her back, and a very fake smile, as if she were waiting for me to yell, "And...cut!" She wore skinny jeans and a pink cashmere sweater with a fitted, shiny, gray puffy vest. I was in yoga pants and a baggy, oversized sweatshirt that read, "Namaste in bed."

We shook hands and made our way to the resort's spa, walking briskly on the limestone trail, which was no easy feat for her in three-inch Jimmy Choo wedges. I'm a girl who knows my shoes—a recovering shoe addict, if you will. I sighed, recalling the days when a $400 pair of shoes was nothing special. I've learned since then. Supporting yourself on a small income and living in an approximately one-hundred square feet space for a year will do that to you.

Darcy got right down to business, her breath fogging up in the brisk air as she peppered me with questions, seemingly oblivious to her ankle precariously turning each time she stepped on a rock.

"So, Emily, tell me—have you had any contact with your dad? When did you find out he was an FBI person of interest?"

"No, I—"

"What's his connection to Elkston's drug runners? Is he a supplier?"

"What? No! No connection that I know—"

"Is the FBI responsible for the explosion? Are they working with the local PD?

"Hang on!" I said, stopping in my tracks. "Slow down." While I was impressed with her ability to speed walk in Jimmy Choos, her endless questioning and frenzied pace were making me anxious, and I was growing irritated.

"I will tell you everything I know, but you have to agree to a few things yourself." She stood there, arms crossed, puffs of breath streaming out of her nostrils like a dragon. "You cannot break this story until I have found my dad and know he's safe. You cannot compromise his identity. You have to be the one to deal with the backlash from the FBI, if there is any. We don't know that he has anything to do with that explosion."

She raised her eyebrows and frowned.

"Well, we don't. He could just be a family deserter for all I know. Maybe he got sick of being a loving husband and father." I shook my head, knowing this wasn't the case. "Regardless, you have to tread lightly. All of this could possibly endanger not only his reputation but also his life." Which was ironic, considering how everyone already thought he was dead. "Please don't be a typical reporter and only care about ratings. Remember you're dealing with actual lives here."

Her investigative reporter façade cracked a little bit, and her shoulders sagged. "Ugh. I do know." She sighed heavily. "Sometimes I forget all about why I wanted to be a reporter in the first place." She laughed quietly, her demeanor changing as we continued walking, our pace slowing considerably. "I used to sit in front of my mirror as a kid and do a skit I called, 'Happy Happenings', where I would report to all of my stuffed animals on the exciting things going on in our neighborhood. It was about sharing fun stories, good news, ya know?" I realized that the plastic, brunette, Barbie-like reporter was opening up to me. Maybe my first impression would need to be modified. Time would tell. "Now all I do is go around trying to find the most sensational stories I can, and in this town, that's no easy feat."

"I get it," I replied, "but please remember—"

"I know, I know. I'll back off a little bit. I don't want to scare you off. You're the best lead I've had in two years." She gave me a lopsided smile as I opened the door to the spa, a smile that was much more genuine than when we first met. I began to relax a bit. I still didn't know if I could trust her, but my fears were slightly allayed.

As we walked into the spa, we were greeted with the delightful scents of lavender and patchouli, just strong enough to be noticed, but not overpowering. Spas always have such a relaxing smell. Unlike most nail salons, this full-service spa did not have TVs in every corner or an overwhelming smell of chemicals. Instead, meditative music played quietly, with the low chatter of women in various stages of nail care in the background. Like the rest of the resort, this had a rustic, log cabin-esque feel with vintage looking manicure stations (though I'm pretty sure manis weren't a "thing" in the late 1800s). The massage rooms and sauna were farther away in the back half of the building, with a gorgeous reclaimed wood wall separating the two areas. Short half-walls of reclaimed wood also separated each pedicure station, and they were just large enough to make the massage chairs and foot spas inconspicuous. A large coffee and cupcake/muffin bar stood at the center of the space and lent a café-like feel. Soon my stomach growled at the sight of the delectable desserts. I'd skipped breakfast since my stomach was tied in knots, and...other things had distracted me as well.

"Good morning, ladies." A tall, lanky woman with waist-long brown hair approached us speaking perfect English, a rarity in some nail salons, per my experience. "My name's Wisteria. I'll walk you right over to your stations."

Darcy and I sat in our massage chairs, side by side, separated by our little half-wall while Wisteria took our coffee and muffin orders. I placed my purse on the floor next to me, making sure I'd have easy access to my phone in case Michael called.

"Coffee. Black. Is it organically, fair trade, shade grown?" Darcy asked Wisteria. "Because if it's not, I'll just take water. Mineral. Assuming you have that." She saw my pointed glare and quickly changed her tone. "Um, you know, scratch that. Whatever kind of coffee you have is fine. And, uh, no muffin, thanks." I could see her gaze longingly at the cupcake and muffin spread, calculating calories.

"Sorry," she whispered to me as Wisteria walked away. "I'm used to—oh, never mind. Sorry." She got herself settled in her chair, and fiddled with the back massage remote, pressing the different buttons. "Ooh, that one tickles. Ouch—what the? Oh yeah, that feels nice." With a satisfied look, she turned to face me.

"So. Are you ready to talk?"

"Hold on," I said, still trying to get comfortable myself. Two small Asian girls who looked no more than thirteen came up and started filling our foot spas. I rarely go to nail salons anymore without my mom around. And when I do, I get so uncomfortable wondering about the ages of the young girls that work there. Are they even of legal working age? With the propensity of young Asian women that don't speak English working at nail salons, I always wonder if they're part of some illegal trafficking ring. I find myself scanning them for bruises or any other signs of abuse and praying they are just girls that are fortunate enough to look ten years younger than they truly are.

"Hi," I said, looking at my nail tech, "how is your day going, uh, Mary?" At least, that's what her nametag said.

She looked up at me with a blank stare. "Color?" she asked quietly and with an accent, handing me the sample palette. "Gel? Super Deluxe?" What were the other options? It wasn't exactly clear, and with no prices posted, I had no idea what I was going to be shelling out, though at this place, it couldn't be cheap. My year spent living frugally made me about as cheap as they come (Michael loves it when I say that). But this time? What the heck. It's my honeymoon. I'd just charge it to the room, or cabin, as it were.

I nodded my assent and pointed out a color. She nodded and carefully placed my feet into the warm, bubbly water. I wiggled my toes, luxuriating in the scent and feel of the bath bomb she dropped in. My feet felt tingly, and the water began to turn a beautiful shade of pink. The massage chair worked its way down my back, kneading out all of the tight spots, and the heat slowly began to radiate through the leather.

Wisteria brought my muffin (chocolate cappuccino) and our coffees (both black) and set them down on the divider. "Enjoy, ladies." She walked off, leaving us to our possibly underage nail techs who may or may not speak English.

"Hey," I whispered, turning to Darcy and offering up the muffin, "you want a bite?"

"Oh, God, no. Not vegan, I'm sure, and definitely not on my diet." She patted her nonexistent belly. "And why are you whispering?" She waved her arms around and spoke loudly to make her point. "They can't understand you."

My eyebrows shot up in embarrassment. I looked around uncomfortably. "How exactly do *you* know?"

"Hellooo? They just...can't. Watch." She turned to face her nail tech, coughing to get her attention.

"So, my boyfriend got his balls shaved the other day, right? Right before he dressed in a tutu and ran screaming around town. Can you believe it?"

The nail tech just looked up and nodded, then went right back down to scrubbing Darcy's feet. I nearly choked on my muffin.

"Okay, fine. I believe you," I said, once I could speak again. "They can't understand us. But still, let's try to keep it down." I looked around at the other people getting treatments, most of whom were staring at their cell phones and not paying attention to anything else. Nobody had even looked our way.

"Of course." Darcy nodded.

"You're not recording this, are you?"

"No."

"Taking notes, then?"

"Up here." She tapped her head. "I have a photographic memory, but for words." She winked.

I'm not sure that's a thing, but I let it go.

The door to the salon opened, and I looked up to see Savannah walk through, giving me a tiny wave as she saw me. I was happy to see they had made it back from the hike yesterday, but she looked exhausted. Her hair, however, was still as perfect as ever. She walked over to quickly say hi and leaned over to see what color I'd selected. We briefly chatted and I introduced Darcy as a friend of mine. She then got seated in a chair not far from us, promptly put in some earbuds and closed her eyes. I was very relieved we wouldn't have to worry about her trying to join our conversation.

I crossed my fingers that Darcy had a code of ethics and would report information cautiously, and spent the next thirty minutes quietly filling her in on my dad's disappearance, presumed death, the scandal surrounding his estate, and the subsequent revelation as an FBI POI. Between gasps and exclamations, she did eventually get out a small notebook and begin jotting down notes. Mary looked up once or twice, but mostly only stared at my feet. I was pretty sure she couldn't understand what we were saying, but I felt uneasy nonetheless. I had a paranoid feeling that someone was listening in.

I told Darcy how I had contracted with Fritz again, and explained our history together, and that Michael was currently picking him up from the airfield.

"I absolutely must meet this guy," she said, nodding her head quickly. "He's going to be a treasure trove of information. He'll be able to get his hands on all kinds of dirt." I could see her forming headlines in her mind.

"Did you bring the footage I need?" I asked.

"Oh, of course." She dug in her purse and handed me a small USB drive. "It's all on there. The video was taken around five yesterday afternoon, and of course, you know the location." I nodded. "The fire marshal is still looking into the cause."

"I thought a gas main leaked?"

"Right, but they're trying to determine why the gas was on, and if the leak was accidental or intentional."

"See, you have no proof my dad's involved at all."

"Hmmm, no, I don't. But my money's on him. Being involved somehow, at least," she added at my look of annoyance. "He might not have blown it up, but he's involved. Did he, uh, happen to have any drug offenses or consort with any known felons?"

"Wha—No! Are you kidding me? He was your average run-of-the-mill dad. He was president of our neighborhood organization, coached my soccer team, volunteered at church, played tennis at the country club." I nearly growled in frustration. Mary looked up briefly and then quickly averted her gaze. "And," I continued, "I haven't spoken to him in alm—"

"I know," Darcy interrupted, "almost two years." She sighed and tapped her pen on her notepad in frustration. "There's got to be a connection." She eyed the remainder of my muffin sitting on its plate. It was so deliciously rich, I had to eat it slowly.

"You want a cupcake or a muffin? I'll get you one." I figured I'd pay for everything anyway since Darcy's local reporter job most likely paid pennies. "We can ask if they have a vegan one. This is Colorado. I'm sure there's a locally sourced, hemp seed cupcake made with beet sugar and...fake butter and...some egg-like product." I gagged a little just envisioning it.

"You know," she sighed, her eyes narrowing, "being a female reporter sucks." She sat back in her chair and crossed her arms, an angry look on her face. "We all have to be perky with perfect bodies and perfect hair and have incredibly big boobs. I'm still paying these off," she said as she looked down at her ample chest. "I have to watch everything I eat. It stinks. And not only that, we're supposed to be wicked smart with a killer instinct. But we can't be too forward, or we're thought of as 'hard to work with.' But a guy can be a jerk and he's just considered 'diligent.' Whatever." She exhaled loudly and closed her eyes. "I just want some chocolate."

I signaled to Wisteria that we'd take another chocolate cappuccino muffin and turned to Darcy. "You know, that double standard doesn't just apply to female reporters." She laughed quietly and nodded. "It pretty much applies to all females in general, sadly." I recalled several of my sorority girls and their sagas of going to formals. They would buy a new, expensive dress and shoes, get a spray tan, and pay to get hair and makeup done. Their dates would show up in khakis, a polo, and sneakers, often already half drunk. Why do guys get off so easy when we are supposed to be 'perfect' and 'sweet?' And why do we, as women, perpetuate it? I thanked God for the millionth time that Michael wasn't like that. He loves me as I am. Flaws, crazy hair, occasional pissiness, and all.

"Screw this," she said when Wisteria brought the muffin over. She took a giant bite, mashing it almost up her nose. "After this, let's go meet up with this Fritz guy and that hubby of yours, and we'll get some lunch. Forget the smoothie today. I'm starving."

I smiled. Maybe Darcy wasn't so bad after all.

• CHAPTER 13 •

AFTER OUR PEDIS WERE FINISHED, we slowly made our way to the restaurant, me in my own flip-flops, Darcy in her millimeter-thick ones provided by the salon. The Jimmy Choo slide-on wedges weren't optimal for newly painted nails.

I thought long and hard about our conversation. I had revealed so much about my dad's situation at the salon and was feeling uncomfortable about it. I had this sense that someone else was watching and listening in, though I saw no indication that anyone was. Maybe I was just being paranoid. Still, I couldn't shake the feeling that I had said too much.

"Did you get the feeling those nail techs were listening to our conversation?" I finally asked Darcy. I hesitated before I continued.

"Whenever they whispered to each other in their native language, I felt like they were talking about us. Do you think they could understand us?"

"Oh, heck no. They don't speak English any more than I speak Chinese...or whatever.

"Could these flip-flops be any thinner? Geez, this hurts!" She cursed the limestone trail and, after about fifty feet of struggling, decided to switch back to the wedges, leaning on me while she carefully changed shoes.

"I actually think it was Korean," I muttered under my breath.

"What was Korean?"

"I think they were speaking Korean. I had a friend that did mission work over there and taught me a few phrases. Anyway," I shook my head, "never mind. I'm sure it's nothing." But still, I had a nagging feeling someone heard more than they should have.

"Right. Hey," she said, one hand on my shoulder, precariously balanced on one foot while she slid the other into the wedge, "check out that guy. Am I wrong, or is that Santa Clause walking around with some hot elf? Damn. I'd take that for Christmas. Mmmm hmmm."

I looked up to see my husband and Fritz walking toward us. Michael towered over Fritz, but what Fritz lacked in height, he made up in girth. I opened my arms wide, leaving Darcy to topple a bit before regaining her balance.

"Fritz!" I exclaimed, giving him a big hug as he walked up. Relief rushed through me and I again realized just how anxious I'd become.

Fritz was dressed in his usual attire of a Hawaiian shirt and cargo shorts with flip-flops. His shirt was red with scattered white flowers. Combined with his snowy white hair and beard and ample belly, he looked like a tropical, jolly old Saint Nick.

"Hey there, kiddo. Where's that snarky reporter?" I had filled Michael in on some of my early morning phone call with Darcy, and he had apparently passed the conversation on to Fritz.

"Excuse me, who are you calling a 'snarky reporter?'" Darcy asked, taking a step forward. She tore her eyes from Michael, planted her hands on her hips and cocked her head.

"The same person who called him a 'hot elf' and me 'Santa Clause.'" Fritz grinned. "Not that I haven't heard it before." He laughed and gave Darcy a hearty slap on the back. "I'm just giving you shit. Fritz McSchatz," he said by way of introduction, sticking out his hand. "Pleased to meet you."

I could see Darcy hesitate at the name and bite her tongue. Thankfully, she composed herself like a true professional and returned the handshake. "I'm very happy to meet you, uh, Mr. McSchatz."

"Oh, God no. It's Fritz. You dare call me Mr. McSchatz and it's off with your head," he grumbled as he turned to face me. Darcy's smile froze and Michael broke in.

"Michael Drake, or, uh, Mr. Emily Drake," he said with a wink in my direction.

"Oh." Her face fell. "Omigod, you guys are too cute," she said in a slightly annoyed voice as he leaned over to give me a kiss. "Sorry about the hot elf comment, I guess. Yes, it's lovely to meet you both."

Fritz reached for my arm. "Emily, I got a phone call this morning from the lab in Houston." We started down the path to the restaurant, Michael and Darcy following a few paces behind us.

"Wow, that was fast. Did they find anything? Any traces of ink?"

"Actually, no."

I frowned but then realized it didn't matter. I had seen my dad on TV. I knew he was alive. The note was irrelevant. I started to say as much to Fritz when he cut me off.

"No ink, but a helluva lot of info anyway."

"What do you mean?" If there was no trace of ink, what was left to find?

"They've seen this stuff before."

"This stuff? As in, the paper?" He nodded. "Okay, and...?"

"It's made from a highly specialized compound, created specifically for the FBI and CIA just a couple of years ago. It's meant to start dissolving once it touches the oil on human hands. Any contact with water only increases the dissolution rate. That's why it turned to goo so quickly."

"You think the guy that gave the note to Father is an agent of some kind? Otherwise, how would he get ahold of that kind of paper?"

"Hell, I don't know," Fritz grumbled, running his hand over his face. "But I think your suspicion in right." He exhaled loudly, puffing his cherry red cheeks out wide.

"Kid, your dad was into some dangerous shit." He put his arm around my shoulders. "You need to brace yourself for this."

"Really, Fritz. After all of this? You think anything's going to surprise me now?"

"Your dad was in deep, Emily."

"You mean, deeply in debt to someone? I thought we got the finances all figured out already. What aren't you telling me?"

"No." Fritz stopped to look at me, concern in his eyes. "Possibly deeply involved in a drug cartel out of Honduras."

My jaw dropped, and I let out a laugh. For the first time, I was beginning to doubt Fritz's investigative abilities. My dad was Mr. Straight and Narrow. He'd never done anything illegal in his life—well, that I knew of anyway.

"My dad would never have had anything to do with drugs, Fritz." Geez! First Darcy, now Fritz. I shook my head. "Bad real estate deals, maybe, but not drugs." I tried to continue walking, but Fritz stopped me.

"Emily, this is real. George Potens was known as *El Diablo Blanco*, The White Devil. The FBI had been tracking his travel patterns for the past several years before his disappearance. He had routinely flown to Honduras, which is one of the biggest drug exporters to the US."

I didn't even know my dad had a passport. He had never traveled outside of the US to my knowledge.

"Well, just because a person travels to Honduras doesn't mean he's a drug dealer." I folded my arms across my chest defiantly. This was insane. "Maybe he was trying to buy land to develop a resort down there. It's a pretty country, isn't it?" I actually know nothing about Honduras. Not a single thing. The geography of other countries isn't my strong suit.

"He'd also been making calls to the head of the Morales Mexican drug cartel. One of the biggest. We're talking the hard stuff, Emily. Cocaine."

Now that wasn't so easy to explain away. What reason could I possibly come up with to explain why my dad was communicating with a drug lord?

"How do you know this?" I stuttered, still unwilling to believe it. "You said his FBI file was mostly redacted." I refused to believe my dad had anything to do with a drug cartel. That was insanity. There had to be a better explanation for all of this.

"I was able to get some of the redacted info in his file...well," he said, shrugging his shoulders, "unredacted."

Michael and Darcy had caught up to us, and I turned around to look at them, my mouth agape. My dad had been communicating with the leader of a drug cartel? He'd been routinely flying to Honduras? How had I not known any of this? Who was he, really? My breathing became shallow and my face flushed. I wanted to crawl into a hole and fall into a deep, deep sleep, only to wake up later and find this had all just been a bad dream. This couldn't possibly be real, could it?

"Woooowww," Darcy said, returning to reporter mode and giving me a little smirk. My good feelings toward her all but evaporated. "I hate to say 'I told you so.'" I felt myself immediately bristle at her remark. Michael reached out to take my hand. Perhaps he knew I was tempted to reach up and smack her across the face as she continued. "This story just got a helluva lot more interesting."

• CHAPTER 14 •

I ENTERED THE RESTAURANT IN A DAZE. A fire crackled in the center of the room, the two-story chimney almost a work of art. Jazz music lightly played through invisible speakers. Hushed conversations and the clinking of silverware were the only other sounds in this peaceful environment. With my head in a fog, my senses seemed to take over. I smelled roast beef, potatoes and gravy, and apple pie. But my stomach was in knots, and, despite the wonderful smells, I no longer had an appetite.

Darcy turned to Fritz and quickly whipped out her notebook to quiz him about what he'd just told us. Apparently, this was too much for her "photographic memory for words."

"Hold on now," Fritz said to Darcy, looking back and forth between the two of us. "Am I supposed to be talking to you? I gotta clear this with the boss first. Emily, you okay with this chick tagging along now?"

Darcy turned red at his comment, and I could see her holding back her anger. Right now, I wasn't her biggest fan, but I was already aggravated and knew I had to say something. I had made a deal with her, after all. And because of her breaking news story, I knew without a doubt that my dad was alive.

"Yes, she's fine," I said, regaining my composure. "And don't call her a 'chick.'"

"Oops. My apologies. I know everyone's getting touchy about things like that nowadays."

Darcy gave me a frustrated look and held up her hands as if to say, *See what I mean?*

"Fritz, you know you're being unfair—"

"I know, I know. Sorry." He held up his hands in the classic surrender pose. "This old codger is stuck back in time. Zoey says I need 'sensitivity training,' or some other BS like that."

"That would be a good start," I snapped. "Lesson one: Take the word 'chick' out of your vocabulary unless you're referring to poultry." He nodded, and to his credit, did look a little chagrined.

Michael asked for a private table near the back, away from most of the other patrons. The hostess sat us in a booth. The benches had cushioned seats and high backs, giving us a sense of privacy. I slid in one side and Darcy immediately followed. That left Michael and Fritz to squeeze in side by side on the other side, their large bodies barely fitting together on the narrow bench seat.

"Let's rearrange," Michael suggested. Fritz got out and Darcy immediately changed places with him, sitting herself comfortably next to Michael. "Not really what I had in mind," he muttered, tilting his head and looking at me. I just shook my head and shrugged it off. She could sit by the "hot elf" during lunch.

Fritz settled in and stretched out his leg into the aisle, moaning. "My sciatica," he said by way of explanation. "Can't hardly stand to sit anymore." He moved around a bit more, adjusting himself until he was comfortable, the bench squeaking and groaning under his weight.

"Okay," he finally said, slapping his hands on the table. "Let's get down to business and watch this video before we discuss this more."

I took the USB from Darcy out of my pocket, and Fritz pulled out his laptop. Getting out his glasses and placing them just below the bridge of his nose, he watched the news clip from the night before with determined interest. He played it several more times, pausing often on different frames to get a better look at my dad. Michael watched it closely as well, his first glimpse of my dad since I'd gotten proof he was alive.

"Okay. Well, that doesn't give me much to go on." Fritz took off his glasses and rubbed his eyes. "I got a decent look at his face though, so that helps." He grilled Darcy about the time the video was shot, how many people were in the area, the owner of the building, and the extent of the damage. As soon as he found out the building was a hotbed for drug activity, he immediately became more animated.

"Well, hot damn. No wonder you got so excited earlier," he said to Darcy, pounding his fist lightly on the table. "This is going to be some fun shit!"

I glared at him. "Trying to find my dad, who you're saying is or was involved in some kind of drug distribution ring, is not going to be 'fun shit!' This isn't fun at all!" He chuckled lightly and patted my arm.

"I know, I know, Emily. I get it, I really do. But I do have some experience with dealers, and I'm certain I'll be able to track some down who know of your dad if he's working around here."

"Do you have a drug dealer database or something?" I asked. It wouldn't surprise me, and I silently wondered if my dad would be in it under some assumed name. "Or just some local contacts? How are you going to find a dealer around here?"

"Oh, I'm pretty sure Caty can help me out." He looked at Michael and they both grinned.

"Caty at the front desk? I don't think drugs are part of room service." I looked at them doubtfully. Fritz just grinned.

"When we walked by her earlier, Emily, the smell of hooch was so powerful, I started to get the munchies." Michael nodded in agreement.

"Okay, but that's legal here," I reminded him.

"Yes, it is. And I want to thank you for bringing me to this great state, by the way." He rubbed his hands together in anticipation. "I'll be able to leave a very happy man." I rolled my eyes. For some reason, his comment didn't surprise me one bit.

Fritz continued. "This afternoon, I'll go pay a visit to Caty and see where I can find the nearest pot shop and then ask where I can get something a little more fun." He looked around the restaurant, taking in the high-end finishes. "People that come here have money to throw around. I bet she's helped her share of guests find their very own 'Rocky Mountain high.'" Fritz slapped his knee at his own joke, then grimaced in pain. "Damn leg! The whole thing hurts!"

Our waiter arrived and we paused our conversation to place our order. I ordered a small bowl of tomato bisque soup and a side salad. I could probably choke that down, though my stomach was protesting. What was my dad thinking? Consorting with drug lords? Taking secret trips to Honduras? How could he have done that for who knows how long and come home to my mom after every trip? How could he have led such a double life? I looked down to see myself clenching my water glass, threatening to break the fine crystal. Silently, I removed my hands to my lap.

As we waited for our food to arrive, I noticed our two nail techs walk in, apparently picking up a to-go order at the bar. And there they stood, speaking perfect English and flirting with the cute bartender. I knew they could understand us!

Mary was telling quite a funny story, apparently. The bartender was doubled over, clutching his belly with laughter. I tried to shut out all other conversation around me and utilize my fabulous lip-reading skills to make out her words.

"Omigod, like, the bitchy one—the reporter lady—was trying to 'prove' that we couldn't speak English. Because, you know, since we're Asian and working in a salon, we must be fresh off the boat. She told this crazy story to see if we'd react. We both just stared at her, and I wanted to say, 'I'm working on my flippin' master's degree in psychology at CSU, and you are a certifiable moron!'"

Her friend smacked her on the shoulder as they all laughed.

"Oh, but wait. The other one apparently is looking for her dad who's been missing for a few years and is wanted by the FBI! And the reporter thinks he's involved in the explosion from yesterday. Seriously! Man, what a pair."

My stomach dropped and I put my head in my hands. They could speak perfect English, and they heard our whole conversation. I glanced up at Darcy, but she was too caught up talking to Fritz and

Michael to even notice. My face burned just thinking about how much had I revealed in the salon. Ugh. This was a nightmare.

Eventually our food came, and I nervously picked at my salad while Darcy continued to grill Fritz on the finer points of being a private investigator. Fritz was more than happy to talk, and when we were all finished, the two of them left the restaurant practically skipping, heads together, as if they were plotting their next move.

Michael pulled me aside as we left, wrapping me in a big hug and creating some distance between us and Darcy and Fritz. Just being in his arms helped me relax. I knew, as long as he was with me, that somehow, everything would be all right. I stared out at the landscape, amazed at how beautiful everything remained while my life turned to chaos. Birds were singing. Leaves were rustling in the wind. The sun's rays warmed my skin. And my dad had possibly worked in the drug trade. Some of the money in my trust fund—the money used for our wedding—could have come from some poor, addicted soul in a back alley. I no longer wanted anything to do with it.

"Hey babe," Michael whispered in my ear, "you know I love you, right?" I went completely still and held my breath. Nothing good ever comes after something phrased like that. "I hate to add to your crazy day, but I've, uh, got some more bad news." I pulled back to look at him. His brow was furrowed and he grimaced as he began to say, "Frit—"

"I tell ya what," Fritz said, turning around and heading back toward us. "Let's all head on back to the room or wherever and talk this out. I need to visit a man about a horse, and then we can sketch out a plan of action." *TMI,* I thought. I wondered how he'd gotten a room at the resort lodge without prior reservations. I knew all the cabins were full and thought the lodge was as well. I'd figured we'd have to find him a place in town.

"Visit a man about a horse?" Darcy mumbled, preoccupied with checking her phone for messages. "Why do you want a horse? You going on a trail ride?"

Fritz looked at her quizzically. "I, uh, need to drop off some kids at the pool?" Darcy still looked confused as she continued to fuss with her phone.

"Huh? There's a pool here too?" she asked. "Awesome!"

Michael looked at me and rubbed his hands over his face, muttering something unintelligible under his breath. "He needs to go to the bathroom, Darcy. That's what he's saying." He gave me an apologetic look. Fritz's bathroom antics were his own business, and this whole conversation was beyond comfortable. "Since that's all cleared up," Michael continued, "why don't we all head back to the cabin."

Why did he say that? I didn't want to invite Fritz to do his business in our cabin. Wouldn't he prefer to go in his own room? I decided I'd better step up and avoid the bathroom disaster.

"Why don't we just take a little break and you can head to your room for a bit, Fritz. Then you can unpack and use your own bathroom and check back in with us when you're done. Take as long as you need." I attempted to herd the group along on our separate ways, my patience waning.

"Ooh, I get my own room? I thought I had the couch?" Fritz said, looking in Michael's direction.

What was he talking about?

"Just come find us when you're done, Fritz," I said, struggling to hide my exasperation. "Do you know where our cabin is?"

"Why, yes." Fritz grinned and continued to follow me. "I certainly do know where *our* cabin is. *Mi casa es su casa,* Emily." He chuckled and patted me on the shoulder. "I'm staying with you."

• CHAPTER 15 •

STAYING WITH FRITZ IS LIKE having an overnight with your favorite uncle. He's lots of fun to be around, but at bedtime, you really wish you'd brought along your earplugs. And your eye mask. And some powerful air freshener.

Turns out a national banker's conference was being held in Elkston, and all hotels, motels, campgrounds, and rooms for rent were booked within a fifty-mile radius. I spent the whole afternoon making calls, even after Michael assured me he'd already done the same thing that morning. It was to no avail, but at least it kept me occupied for a bit.

Eventually, Michael and I lit a fire and sat on the sofa, which was soon to become Fritz's bed. I sighed in frustration. The room was nice and cozy, sun streaming in behind us with the fire crackling at our toes. Darcy and Fritz worked in the kitchen area just behind us, both situated at the table, heads together, almost speaking their own language. It turned out Darcy had quite a knack for investigative reporting and had quite a few contacts of her own. The two had their laptops, phones, and notes spread out, fingers flying from one device to the other, stopping occasionally to make a phone call. So much for our romantic honeymoon sanctuary.

"I had high hopes for this sofa," Michael whispered, giving me a sad face. "It's comfortable, pretty deep, right in front of the fire. I guess we'll just have to put this spot on hold for a few days."

"What are you talking about?" I asked as I leaned against him, curling my legs up underneath me. My brain was buzzing trying to think of other places I could call to check on room availability for Fritz.

"You know I wanted to christen every room of this cabin on our honeymoon." He kissed me on the cheek.

"Oh, right. That." I laughed. Why do men have such one-track minds? "I'm happy to see you're so focused on finding my dad. You're going to have to wait a few days for any of that, or at least until we find Fritz a different place to stay."

"Wait, what? A few days?" Michael gulped and shifted to look at me. He looked like he'd lost his best friend. "Are you serious? We're on our honeymoon!"

"And I'm not doing the dirty deed with Fritz one room away and a sliding barn door the only thing separating us."

"What about the SUV?"

"Are you kidding me right now?"

"Hey, maybe I'm just trying to lighten the mood," he teased as he stroked my face. "I know this isn't what we planned." He sat and gazed at the fire, a sad look of defeat in his eyes.

"Oh, I forgot," he said with a start. Turning to look at his watch, he stood up, pulling me with him. "I had made reservations for the two of us to get a couples massage this afternoon. If we hurry up, we can still get in a short hike around the property beforehand."

"We're just going to leave?" I looked at Darcy and Fritz working away at the table. "I feel like we should be doing something."

"We are," Michael said, looking at me with eyes full of love. "We're getting out of their way. And you will be forced to relax." He wrapped his hands around my waist. "Which is just what you need." He tipped his forehead down to touch mine, letting his hands slowly slide down my hips and around to cup my—

"Good Lord, can't you two keep your hands off each other for five seconds?" Fritz looked up at us with a sly grin. "Caught ya, didn't I?" Darcy rolled her eyes and smacked his arm before she sat back in her chair and let out a big yawn, stretching her arms overhead.

"Give them a break. They're on their honeymoon." She stood up to make herself some tea with the Keurig. "And you need to stay on task. I feel like something's about to break wide open. Focus." She returned to her laptop, fingers pounding away.

"Yes, mom," Fritz responded, shaking his head. He stood up to stretch out, wincing at the pain from his sciatica shooting down his leg.

"You have any luck finding me a room elsewhere?"

I shook my head no.

"Well, shit. I hate to ruin your honeymoon." He paused and rubbed his beard, looking toward the bedroom. "That barn door doesn't look very soundproof." Michael tried unsuccessfully to suppress a grin while sticking his chest out like a proud rooster. I blushed. "I think I've got some earplugs in here somewhere," Fritz said as he dug around in his duffel bag.

"Awkward," Darcy mumbled quietly, keeping her gaze averted.

"Ah, found 'em." Fritz held up some bright orange earplugs with a look of triumph. "You kids have all the fun you want. Get a couple of beers in me, and with the help of these puppies, I shouldn't hear a thing. Just maybe try to keep it down a little." He sat back down and continued working, as though blatantly talking about my sex life was all in a day's work.

Michael and I threw on some hiking shoes and went out to explore the property before heading to the spa for a massage. The fall Colorado weather could not have been more perfect. The sun was shining brightly overhead and there was just enough of a breeze to cause the gorgeous yellow aspen leaves to rustle lightly. The cool, brisk air was invigorating. The tall peaks of the mountains rose up behind us while the town of Elkston spread out peacefully in the valley below. It was hard to imagine such a beautiful place had its own share of problems, just like everywhere else. Violence, crime, drugs—the latter possibly thanks to my own dad.

I didn't know how to handle my emotions. They kept swinging from one extreme to another. Elation over the thought that my dad was alive. Anger and disgust at the thought of him being a drug smuggler and lying to me and my mom for all these years. My dad had been a good man...or so I thought. He raised me to be responsible and hardworking (okay, I admit that took a while longer than it should have). My mom ran charities, helped the homeless, and raised and gave loads of money to local nonprofits. She's the one who found a speaker to come talk to my eighth grade class about saying no to drugs! How could my dad reconcile himself to the life he was leading? The hypocrisy of it all made me crazy.

"Babe, uh, can you loosen your grip just a bit?" I looked down at my hand squeezing Michael's and immediately relaxed my hold.

"Sorry." I sighed, taking it all in. I stared down at the valley. "My dad is somewhere down there. I just can't believe it."

"We'll find him."

"Right. And then what do I say when we do? 'Oh, hey Dad, I thought you were dead! Thanks for not contacting me for eighteen months. And, by the way, what the hell were you doing in Honduras all those years, and what's up with those Mexican drug cartel friends of yours?!' I can't even imagine the conversation. Really! What am I going to say to him?"

"Maybe he can explain it all away," Michael said, stopping and pulling me close. He circled his arms around my waist and held me to him. "Maybe there really is a good reason behind all of this."

"You're too damn optimistic," I said into his chest. "I'm a realist."

Michael laughed. "I wouldn't say I'm optimistic so much as I'd rather stay on the good side of my father-in-law until I know all of the facts. You're his daughter, and he'll love you no matter what. He doesn't know me from Adam."

"You're right," I said, a thought suddenly popping into my head. "He doesn't know you." I started to pull away, looking up at his face. "You can help Fritz look for him."

"Well, sure I can, but—"

"He doesn't know your face. After all, he probably wasn't at the wedding at all. He doesn't know Fritz. But if he's been here any length of time, he might recognize Darcy from TV, and of course he'd know me."

"I get it, but—"

"We'll have to split up. You two go into town asking around at coffee shops, gas stations, grocery stores. Take his picture and ask if anyone's seen him. If they know where he might be staying." I let go of his hands and started pacing. "Darcy and I will keep looking into the drug connection here and see what we can come up with." I rolled my eyes. "God, I can't believe I just said that about my own *father.*"

"Babe, I'll do whatever it takes to try and find your dad. You know I will. But we have to be careful here." Michael ran a hand through his hair, his brow furrowed. "If your dad's involved in the drug community and he or anyone else thinks someone's after him...well, we just have to tread lightly."

I took a deep breath and sighed, my hands falling to my sides. He was right. I was getting ahead of myself. I needed to slow down. But tension coursed through my veins, making that nearly impossible. "I know. I'm just so antsy to get moving. I can't sit here much longer while Darcy and Fritz data mine, or whatever it's called. We've got to physically start looking."

"And we will," Michael said, reaching for my hand, "in exactly one hour and thirty minutes. Right now, let's take advantage of this elite resort we're staying at and go get our couples massage." He smiled down at me, and I couldn't help but grin back. He was right. For the next hour and a half, I'd try really hard to banish the mystery of my dad's whereabouts to the back of my mind and let Fritz worry about it. It was only ninety minutes. I could do that, right? I was going to forget about everything and relax and enjoy a deep tissue massage right next to my sexy, loving husband. I took a deep breath to clear my head. Man, I was lucky. I just hoped, in the next few days, that my luck wouldn't run out.

• CHAPTER 16 •

OUR MASSAGES WERE INCREDIBLE, and I didn't want to leave when our time was up. A ninety-minute massage always seems to fly by so quickly. One minute I'm lying there, listening to the relaxing spa music, falling into a near trance as my muscles are expertly kneaded. The next minute they're telling me they're all finished and it's time to go. Michael and I languished side by side while our massage therapists left the room to give us time to get dressed.

"You're looking pretty sexy there all oiled up," he whispered in his deep voice, smiling mischievously and slowly starting to sit up from the table. He lifted his arms overhead and stretched, flexing the muscles in his well-toned upper body. "What do you say we head back to the cabin and..." His face fell and he dropped his hands.

"Crap. I forgot all about who was waiting for us back there. Dammit, dammit, dammit. My wife is naked and oiled up right next to me." He groaned quietly and put his head in his hands. "And I can't do anything about it. Ugh. Life is cruel. I need a cold shower."

I smiled and looked at my beautiful husband, clearly in a special kind of physical agony.

"Well...like you said, we always have the SUV," I whispered back at him. I got up from the table and let the sheet slowly drop to the floor. His head shot up.

"I thought you didn't—"

"Maybe I changed my mind. We didn't tell Darcy and Fritz when we'd be back, so...maybe we have to run into town for a few things...and maybe it takes a little longer than we expected." I winked at him as a smile formed on his face. "I'm sure we can find some back road to, you know, have a little quiet time together."

"You're on," he whispered huskily, getting up and pulling me to him for a slow, deep kiss. I didn't want to stop, but the knock on the door from my therapist, telling me she had a glass of water waiting, brought me back to reality. Michael finally pulled back and I looked down and tilted my head.

"I don't know how you walk around with that thing."

He let out a belly laugh and kissed the top of my head before looking deep into my eyes. "Race ya!" he said, releasing his grip and reaching for his clothes.

I swiftly grabbed my yoga pants and sweatshirt, pulling them on and beating him by a good thirty seconds as he struggled to zip his jeans. "That's not fair," he said, looking down. "I have an extreme disadvantage."

"Oh, poor you." I gave him a sad face and threw my hair in a ponytail. "I'll be sure to make it up to you."

We walked out of the room hand in hand and got our tiny cups of water from the massage therapists before heading outside. We briskly walked back toward the cabin to get the SUV. I texted Fritz and told him we had to run into town for a few things. He texted back, *Food...beer.* I felt bad that they'd been holed up working while we'd been hiking around and getting massages, so I made a mental note to pick up something really yummy to eat.

We got in the SUV, and Michael peeled out of the parking spot before I even had my seatbelt on.

"You in a hurry?" I asked with a grin.

He looked at me and smiled deviously. "As a matter of fact, I am."

I put my head on his shoulder and slowly walked my hand up his leg. He let out a low groan and pressed hard on the gas before immediately easing up. "Damn winding mountain roads." He navigated the twists and turns like a pro, commenting to himself that he should have been a race car driver.

Halfway down the mountain, we came across an abandoned mining road. The sun was starting to set behind the trees, and we saw no signs of life in the area. Michael took the turn and carefully drove around a rusted gate with a faded "No Trespassing" sign dangling by a nail.

"Why did you turn here?" I whispered, pointing at the sign. "It says 'No Trespassing.'"

"Emily, that sign's ancient, this road looks deserted, and I really, really can't hold out much longer. If you'd get your hand off my leg...maybe."

I pulled my hand back.

"Kidding," he said with a smirk. "Too late." He stopped the SUV about 100 yards from the turnoff. The area was completely overgrown, and we could hardly see the main road. The light from the setting sun barely filtered through the dense tress, and we sat in near darkness. Michael turned off the vehicle and turned toward me.

"Are you sure no one can see us here?" I giggled, feeling like a teenager.

"I don't really care," he said, taking my face in his hands and kissing me.

"Michael!" I swatted his chest, feigning annoyance.

"I promise you no one is watching us," he said, taking my hand and kissing my fingertips one by one. His eyes were dark and his gaze was intense. I felt heat course through my body and my heart began to quicken at his touch. The windshield immediately started to fog up. "Now come on over here and let's finish what your oiled up, relaxed, naked body lying next to me started." He moved his seat back, pulled me into his lap, and erased everything else from my mind.

A little while later, I lay contentedly on Michael's chest, breathing in the scent of him. I wanted to stay like this forever and not have to head back out to the real world full of secrets and lies.

"I don't want to go back," I mumbled into his shirt. I was perfectly content where I was. "I want to stay right here and take a nap."

Michael laughed his deep laugh, and I could feel it vibrate through my body, making me smile. I put my chin on his chest and sighed.

"Well, we definitely have to remember this spot for as long as we have houseguests the rest of this week. But hey, I'll make you a deal," he said, turning on his side and cradling me to him in our cramped quarters. "We'll run into town real quick, and you can stay in here and get your nap while I run in somewhere and pick up food and beer. Sound good?"

I looked up at him and grinned. He's such a good man. Always making sure I'm happy and content. "You're so sweet to me. How did I get so lucky?"

Michael sighed and stretched his arms overhead. "Luck had nothing to do with it, babe. This was fate."

I was reminded of the Halloween party at my old sorority house nearly a year ago before we'd started dating. I'd worn an old bridesmaid's dress and gone as the Bride of Frankenstein. Michael showed up, completely unaware of my outfit, as Frankenstein himself. He'd said almost the exact same thing back then. It was fate. We were meant to be together.

I gave him a quick kiss and slowly crawled back over to my side of the SUV. He started it up and, once we were both settled, we began slowly creeping back down the abandoned road toward the intersection. It was completely dark by now, and had we gone much further into the forest, we might have lost the road completely. As it was, our headlights just barely made out the old gate signaling the intersection, and the SUV rumbled toward it.

Just as we approached the main road, a large black truck with blinding headlights veered around the gate, zoomed past us, and raced up the abandoned road, narrowly missing our bumper. Michael slammed on the brakes, jerking us back.

"Where the hell did that come from?" he asked in surprise. "You okay?"

"Yeah? You?" My heart was racing at the near miss. "Did you see who that was?" Michael shook his head. The truck had flown by us, but as it turned, our headlights had clearly shone on some serious helmet head. "It was Dirk and Savannah. What do you think they're doing out here?"

"I don't know," Michael said, pulling out on the main road after looking each direction twice, "but he was flying." He looked at me and smirked. "You think we're not the only ones that need a place to get away? There's absolutely nothing down that road."

Blood rushed to my face as I realized just how close we'd come to being caught in a compromising position. We had to find another place for Fritz to stay.

As my heart rate settled down, I checked some local hotels on my phone again, hoping for a cancellation, but still saw no vacancies. Hoping I'd have better luck tomorrow, I put it out of my mind and instead looked up local restaurants and called in an order at a barbecue place.

We continued down the mountain and drove into town. Michael stopped at a local brewery and bought a few six-packs of their seasonal ales – Pecan Ale, Octoberfest, and Hard Apple Cider. I stayed in the car, sinking down in the seat, trying to look incognito while surreptitiously stealing glances at people walking by, hoping to get a glimpse of my dad. I knew it was a long shot. But if I did see him, what would I do? In my heart, I knew I'd run up and hug him and not let him go. But if he saw me without me knowing it, he was likely to hightail it out of town. He'd made that much clear by never trying to find me in the first place after he'd disappeared. I knew I had to be the one to find him. I couldn't risk him seeing me accidentally and fleeing.

Next, we swung by the barbecue place and picked up our food before heading back to the cabin. Everything smelled delicious and my stomach growled in anticipation. Sitting in the car with the food in my lap all the way back up the mountain was pure torture.

The warmth of the fire greeted us as we walked inside the cabin. The firewood had been replenished, and Darcy and Fritz remained focused on their work at the table. The only difference from earlier was that Darcy's hair was now falling out of a loosely tied ponytail, and Fritz had changed from a Hawaiian shirt and cargo shorts into a white T-shirt and Parrothead sweatpants.

Darcy was very quiet and intent, eyes focused on the screen, a serious and somber look on her face. Fritz, however, had turned on some Doobie Brothers, and was alternating between playing the air guitar and using his hands to pound out the beat of the drums on the table.

"Will you stop that and turn off the prehistoric music, please?" Darcy finally asked when Fritz's mock drumming landed some of her notes on the floor. She threw her hands up in frustration. "I'm trying to work here!"

"My bad, my bad," Fritz said, leaning over to pick up the fallen papers. "I'm not used to working with other people around. That's the benefit of a one-man shop." He fished some earbuds out of his bag and took them out of their case. "I do keep a pair of these things on hand for flights and such, when people might not share my fine taste in music." He gave Darcy a pointed glare while he struggled to put them in, fishing around through a forest of ear hair before getting them just right. "That good?" he yelled.

Darcy gave him a thumbs up as the music disappeared and continued to type away.

"Oh Mississippiii, she's hmmm hmmm hmmm hmmm," Fritz quietly sang out, head bopping, as he jotted down some notes of his own.

Darcy dropped her head and let out a low growl. Michael set the beer down on the counter, put his hands over his ears, and walked to the bathroom. I giggled quietly at Fritz's inability to stay on tune. He was ruining a good song.

"I'd like to hear some doodoo doodeedoo, pretty momma, doobeedoobeedoobeedoo."

Darcy coughed out loud in an attempt to get Fritz's attention.

"...hand...pretty momma! Gonna bambambah banaa aaall night long."

"Omigod, I'm done here," Darcy said, slamming her laptop shut and standing up. "I need to get going anyway." She grabbed her vest and put it back on, winding her scarf around her neck.

"No barbecue and beer?" I asked, holding up the bags of food.

"Nope. I already spoiled my diet earlier." She sniffed the air though and sighed out loud, as if she relished the smell of real food. "A wheatgrass smoothie is calling my name," she said reluctantly.

As I walked her out, I discreetly asked her if she possibly had a spare bedroom, shooting furtive glances at Fritz.

"Ha! Not on your life," she responded. "Nice try though. I feel for you, I really do." She turned to look at Fritz as we got to the door. "But I have to get some sleep, and I have a feeling he sounds like a freight train when he snores." Putting her hand on my arm, she squeezed it gently. "Good luck with that."

• CHAPTER 17 •

FRITZ, MICHAEL AND I CLEARED the table before spreading the food out. Michael found a bottle opener and cracked open a few beers. Hard Apple Cider is my personal favorite. Fritz chose Pecan Ale, and Michael tried the Octoberfest.

"You guys look like you've had a rough time of it," Fritz commented. Michael and I both froze, and I did a mental assessment of things I might have in my hair that would give away what we'd done in the SUV. But I came up with nothing.

"I mean, you both look exhausted."

I exhaled in relief. "I am exhausted, Fritz," I admitted, pouring barbecue sauce on my pulled pork. "All of these unknowns regarding my dad...well, it's driving me nuts. I'm not sleeping well at all. It's all I can think about."

"Surely that's not the only reason you're not sleeping well," he said, slapping Michael on the back and causing him to choke, "but I get it." He shook his head, getting serious. "This would stress anyone out.

"Darcy and I did some digging earlier and didn't net a whole lot." Putting a half rack of ribs on his plate, he continued. "I'm having a helluva time getting more info in those files unredacted. The FBI has really clamped down on them. My sources—and you know I don't like to work with the feds—are hitting roadblocks everywhere." He began tearing into the ribs. "Oh yeah, this is some good stuff," he commented. "Mmmm. Mmmm. Mmmm." Barbecue sauce soon coated his mustache and beard.

I gave him a few minutes to eat in silence, marveling at the amount of food he and Michael could shovel in. I can throw down a decent amount of food myself, but sometimes watching the amount of food others can eat makes me feel ill. Fritz was no exception. Ribs, mashed potatoes, beans, fries, corn, Texas toast...and then he asked if we had any dessert. I shook my head no.

"That's ok. I'll have some Hard Apple Cider for my dessert. You got any Fireball to go with this? No? Okay." He sat back and rubbed his belly, exhaling with satisfaction.

"Darcy did find some good dirt though on the guy who owns the building that was destroyed."

"Really?" I asked, wiping my plate clean with the last piece of toast. I still didn't want to believe my dad had anything to do with that explosion, but it seemed to be the avenue those two were taking. "What did she find?"

Fritz stretched out his bad leg and winced a bit. Michael stood up and began cleaning up dishes.

"Well, turns out the company that owns it is a shell company called C-IZZY. She was able to trace that to an individual listed as C.C. Isaguirre out of Matamoras, Mexico. My intel shows this Isaguirre—Izzy, I guess—is messed up in some pretty bad stuff and is famous for evading authorities and remaining a virtual ghost. No one knows what he even looks like."

"Why would someone from Matamoras own an abandoned building in Elkston, Colorado?"

"Well, that's a good question. We did some more digging, and Izzy owns quite a few derelict properties in high-end resort towns such as this one." Fritz let out a loud burp and pounded on his chest. Classy.

Michael brought over more beers for the three of us and sat back down. "Okay, but what does that have to do with Emily's dad?"

"Izzy just happens to be connected to the Morales cartel out of Matamoras."

"Oh, great," I said. "Let me guess. Izzy distributes cocaine to these resort areas."

Fritz pointed at me, nodding his head slowly. "Bingo. That's the theory, at least."

I let out a slow breath. "Great. So, you think my dad's here to strike up a deal with him?" I shook my head at the thought. "But then why would he blow up one of his buildings? Isn't that just asking for trouble?"

"It is." He nodded, frowning.

"You think maybe he's working for this guy? Maybe they wanted to destroy the building for insurance money?" I was grasping at straws here, still in denial that we were even having this conversation.

"That building is valued at $248,000, which is a lot of money, but that's chump change to a drug cartel that deals in billions. Plus, I don't think they'd want to draw attention to themselves that way."

"So either my dad had nothing to do with it or he's asking for trouble."

"I'm afraid so," Fritz sighed, stroking his beard. "A man with possible drug ties who's been in hiding for this long shows up at the scene of an explosion of a building owned by someone connected to one of the biggest drug cartels in Mexico. Unless it was a total accident...I'd say he's asking for trouble."

I went to bed that night with no more answers than I'd woken up with. What the hell was my dad involved in? At this point, I pretty much knew my mom was not in the picture, and it crushed me. I knew with all of my heart that she would have tried to find me if she were still alive. And I was becoming more and more convinced that the one-car accident on the highway in the bayou of Louisiana was not an accident at all. They'd been targeted, and somehow my dad had escaped.

I could feel the anger in my veins making my blood boil. Fritz's snoring from the couch in the living room only exacerbated my irritation. I tossed and turned all night, intermittent nightmares the only proof I had slept a wink.

Morning came, and I hurriedly got out of bed at the first sign of light. I couldn't try to force sleep any longer. Putting on some leggings and a long sweatshirt, I grabbed my tennis shoes, gloves, and a cap and headed outside for a quick jog to clear my mind. I snatched my cell phone and slipped it in a pocket. Putting earbuds in, I pulled up some classic heavy metal, hoping to pound the anger out one way or another. I didn't have a punching bag but sure could have used one.

Sticking to the road, I started to wind my way down the mountain, not even considering that I'd have to haul my ass back up it later. It was such a gorgeous morning...again. Far too bright and cheery to suit my mood. I was hoping that the fresh air and physical exercise would clear my head somewhat and release the stress hormones building up inside of me.

I jogged down the hill about a mile before coming to a clearing just off the side of the road. Stopping to catch my breath, I forced myself to take in the beauty of my surroundings. I walked into the clearing and found a smooth rocky outcrop on which to sit. Stretching out my legs, I did some light hamstring stretches before standing back up and going through a series of yoga sun salutations.

The sun peeked out over the ridge and shone brightly over the landscape, making the light frost on the grass and brush glitter. Everything was absolutely gorgeous. I took out my phone and snapped a few pictures, hoping to capture the beauty of the moment. I wanted to remember this part of the trip—the tranquility, the amazing scenery, and the peacefulness—not the worry, panic, suspicion, and haunting questions.

I laid back on the rocks and basked in the sun for a few more minutes, taking it all in before getting back up and considering the daunting task of running one mile back up the mountain. I had a feeling it would be more of what Lisa calls a "slog"—slow jog. That incline looked pretty steep going back up. Gritting my teeth, I put on some slower paced music, got myself ready for a serious ass and quad workout, and began my ascent.

Just as I hit the road, I saw a black truck winding its way slowly down the hill. It looked just like the truck we had seen last night after our hurried rendezvous. Sure enough, Dirk was at the wheel. He did a double take when he saw me, pulled off the road, and rolled down his window. He waved at me with his hugely muscled arm, a barbed wire tattoo snaking down and around his nicely toned forearm.

"Hey, there!" Savannah called, leaning over, looking very perky for so early in the morning. Her makeup was perfect, hair curled and helmeted into place. I wondered just how many hours it took her to get ready in the morning. Maybe she primped while Dirk lifted weights. "You doing some sightseeing early this morning?"

"Just getting in a morning run," I replied, walking up to the truck. "It's so pretty out."

"Where's your honey?"

"Probably still sleeping. I couldn't sleep, so I kind of snuck out. I'm just on my way back up the mountain."

"Want a ride?" Dirk asked.

"Uh, aren't you on your way down?" I grinned and tapped my finger on his forearm. Yep, rock solid.

"Oh, yeah, I guess we are." He chuckled and shifted uncomfortably. Savannah swatted him lightly on the arm.

"Darlin', you are so silly. I swear!" Shifting her gaze back to me, she brushed an invisible strand of hair behind her ear. "So did you see anything good on your way down? Any signs of life? We've noticed it's pretty remote up here. No other buildings or anything besides the resort."

I shook my head. "To be honest, I really wasn't looking for signs of life. Trying to focus on nature, I guess." I glanced at the mountainside, seeing only trees, shrubs, and fallen rocks. "I'd guess there aren't any houses up here, unless they're pretty well hidden."

"Yeah," she sighed almost wistfully, "maybe." Her demeanor changed and she was quiet for a moment, staring out the window as if in a daze. She shook her head and the smile returned. "Well, if you do notice anything, be sure to let us know. You know we're in the market and Dirk's just fallen in love with this place." She playfully kissed his cheek and patted his leg.

"Will do. Well, I'd better get back. Nice seeing you two."

I stepped back from the truck, and they continued down the mountain. Maybe they were out looking for properties in the dark last night? Perhaps the land around that abandoned road was for sale? A blush crept up my face as I again thought of how close we'd come to being caught in the act, and I giggled to myself.

I slogged the rest of the way up the mountain, stopping only two times to catch my breath. It took me twice as long to jog up as it had to jog down, but I still considered it a small victory. Plus, I no longer had the energy to be as agitated as I'd been before. Win, win.

I opened the door to the cabin and was greeted with the smells of an already cooked breakfast. It was heavenly. A nice spread of food was carefully set out on the kitchen counter. Eggs, sausage, pastries, toast, and cut-up fruit lay in their respective to-go containers, and the smell of freshly brewed coffee filled the air.

Fritz was piling his plate high, dressed in a white fluffy robe that I'm pretty sure was one of the complimentary robes that had been hanging in the bathroom. On his feet were fuzzy black slippers that looked as if they'd seen better days.

"I took the liberty of ordering in from the resort's kitchen while you were out," he said. "This place has some good grub, and they're crazy fast."

Michael walked out of the bedroom in his flannel pajama bottoms, rubbing his eyes. "Y'all wake up way too early," he said with a yawn. He did a double take when he saw Fritz. "Nice robe, man. Pretty sure my wife wore that yesterday."

Fritz chuckled and put his plate down. "Sorry about that, Emily. You want it back?" He began to untie the belt and open the robe. I wasn't sure what Fritz was wearing underneath that robe, if anything, but I really didn't want to find out. My hands flew up and I quickly whipped my eyes up toward the ceiling.

"Nope! I'm good. Really. Just keep it on. Please, I insist." He shrugged his shoulders and acquiesced, belting the robe back into place and sitting down at the table with his plate.

"Darcy texted me in the middle of the night to say she'd found some info and is going to come over as soon as she's off the air this morning." He grabbed the saltshaker and began dousing his eggs with it. "I think she's found something on the infamous C-IZZY."

"Did you ever get down to talk to Caty?" I asked.

"Nope. I didn't get there yesterday afternoon, and she wasn't there when I phoned the front desk this morning. The person I spoke with acted like she comes in when she wants to. Damn millennials," he muttered. "I don't know how you run a successful business like that. Employees just coming in whenever they want to."

Michael got three mugs out of the cupboard and poured us all a generous amount of coffee.

"G'morning, sunshine," he said, kissing my cheek. "Why'd you get up so early?"

"Eh, I couldn't sleep." Story of my life, lately, it seemed. "So I went for a jog. Saw Dirk and Savannah on their way into town."

"Man, we keep seeing them," he commented, winking at me. Another blush rose to my cheeks, remembering last night. "You check out Dirk's biceps as they drove by?"

"As a matter of fact, they stopped so I could get in a nice squeeze," I said, teasing him. "Actually, I think they were out looking at properties around here. We just chatted for a second."

I grabbed a plate and helped myself to a pastry, a piece of sausage, and some fruit. Michael loaded his plate up to rival Fritz's, and together we sat at the table to eat.

"I wouldn't think there'd be much property for sale around here," Fritz said before putting a forkful of eggs in his mouth. "Wouldn't it all be owned by the state or part of some preserve?" He looked at us and shrugged. "Hell, I haven't a clue who owns these mountains."

Michael cut his croissant before stuffing it with eggs and sausage and dousing it with hot sauce. "If it's not in the national park or part of the national forest, it could easily be private land. I mean, surely this resort is on private land."

"I guess so," Fritz agreed. "But just for the hell of it, let's look it up." He got up and puttered over to his laptop, the robe gaping open as he squatted down to pick it up along with his glasses. I quickly turned away until he was back at the table, robe safely closed. Michael spit out some coffee trying to hold back a laugh.

"Let's see here." Fritz set down his laptop and booted it up. He grabbed a piece of toast, buttered it, and slathered it with jam. "I'm going to see if I can pull up the county assessor's website, and maybe a real estate site or two. What county are we in, anyway?"

None of us had any idea of the county name, so Fritz Googled it and then opened up the local county assessor website. He typed in the physical address of the resort and waited a beat.

"Really?" he muttered to himself, looking at the screen. His fingers moved swiftly as he kept typing. "Hmmm, well, you gotta be..." He shook his head in frustration, hit a few more keys and landed his elbows on the table, rubbing his beard. "This is going to take some time."

"What's the problem?" I asked from across the table. I finished the last sip of my coffee and stood up to get more. Walking around the table, I glanced at his screen and noticed several windows open. "Not finding what you're looking for?" Filling my cup, I walked back around the table, lazily running my hands across Michael's shoulders before sitting back down.

"You could say that," Fritz mumbled, concentrating on the display. His eyes darted from one window to the next.

Michael yawned, stood up, and began picking up dishes. The man had packed down that whole plate in something like sixty seconds. "I'm going to clean up real quick and get a quick shower." His eyes caught mine and he started motioning between the two of us. *"You wanna join me?"* he mouthed.

I smirked at him and shook my head, knowing there was no way we could pull that off with the bathroom right off the open concept area in which we were sitting. He lowered his head in a mock pout and continued to put the food away.

"Holy..." Fritz muttered, fingers flying. "Are you kidding me? There's no way..." His eyes moved back and forth, scanning the information he'd pulled up. I could see him skimming through the pages as quickly as he could, brow furrowed, lips pursed. Finally, he shook his head and lifted his gaze just above the glasses perched low on his nose.

"You're not going to believe this," he said, sitting back. He took off his glasses and rubbed his eyes. "C-IZZY owns the whole thing."

"C-IZZY owns the resort?" I asked in surprise.

"Not just the resort," Fritz continued. "C-IZZY owns the whole damn mountain."

• CHAPTER 18 •

MY CELL PHONE RANG, THE SHRILL NOISE jerking us all out of our stupor. I yanked it out of my pocket and looked at the screen.

"It's Darcy," I said. I got up from the table and walked into the sitting area. One of my pet peeves is people talking extra loud on a cell phone right in my face, so I prefer not to do it to others.

"Hey, Darcy, what's up?"

"I just got off the air," she said hurriedly. She sounded like she was shuffling papers around. "I have a few more things to catch up on here, then I'm bailing out early and planning to drive out to your place. I texted Fritz but wanted to check with you. You good with that?"

"Yeah, come on over." I looked back at Fritz who gave me a quick thumbs up as his fingers kept clacking against the keyboard.

"Tell her to bring her hiking boots," he yelled over his shoulder.

"Uh, hiking boots?" I said to him, covering the mouthpiece. "Darcy already told me she doesn't own any. Why would she need them anyway?"

"Well, she needs to get her ass to the store then and buy some." He looked up at me with a sly grin. "That man owns the whole mountain, Emily, and I have a funny feeling about it. So I figure we might as well do some exploring."

While Michael and I both showered—separately—Fritz came up with a plan to start investigating the C-IZZY properties as if we were just interested in them from a real estate perspective. According to the county assessor website, the mountain was divided up into five distinct parcels, and one of them held a very large house nestled so far back into the property that an image of the actual structure wasn't available. However, the barebones footprint was online, as well as the aerial photo. The other parcels, besides the resort, appeared to be vacant of any structures.

Michael pulled me aside into the bedroom after my shower and slid the barn door shut. My hair was still wet, and I was wearing his robe, since Fritz had taken mine. I reached up and held it shut tight at the neck, playfully swatting his arm away.

“Not now,” I said, in mock disapproval. “Can’t you give a girl a break? Fritz is right behind that door.”

“Babe, I didn’t pull you in here for that.” His face grew concerned, and he ran his hand across his face. “I don’t like the path we’re taking here.” He pulled me down to sit on the bed and rubbed his hands up and down his thighs as if he were nervous. “I don’t like to tell you what to do. I know you’re very independent and don’t like to be bossed around.” He paused and looked at me so tenderly, my heart melted. “You were in danger the last time we went along with one of Fritz’s schemes, and I can’t take that chance again.” Taking my hand, he continued. “I will go with Fritz to snoop around, but I don’t want you anywhere nearby.”

“Aw, babe.” I wrapped my arms around him and leaned into him. The last time I went along with one of Fritz’s ideas, I had inadvertently almost gotten myself killed. The whole thing scared Michael so badly, he proposed soon after, and had barely left my side since. “I get it. I really do.”

I had to respect my husband’s wishes. But I also had to find my father. And if Fritz thought searching Izzy’s properties might help... Ugh. I just didn’t know what to do. If I backed out and sent Michael and Fritz alone, I’d just be putting them in danger, wouldn’t I? But then I laughed at my own thinking. My husband is built like a fortress. He’s strong, tough, and wickedly smart. If he’d been in that fateful room with Shiner and a gun last year, he'd have disarmed him in ten seconds flat. I have no doubt about that. But Fritz...

The thought of me hanging back was one thing. However, I was also beginning to feel hesitant about Darcy tagging along with them. She's basically a local celebrity and an occasional investigative reporter to boot. She might be easily recognized, and the thought of her possibly showing her face to someone connected to a local drug supplier didn't sit well with me. If someone recognized her, it might set off alarm bells and put them all in danger, not to mention ruin any chance of finding my dad.

Maybe she and I could still help out by doing some investigating of our own remotely, from right here. Maybe Darcy had some connections she could check out, and I could go talk to Caty while the guys drove around to different properties. I didn't know how I was going to pull off pretending I wanted to score some drugs, but I guess I'd just have to work on my acting skills.

I turned to Michael and gave him a smile. "You're right. I think maybe Darcy and I should both hang back." I explained my reasoning and felt him immediately relax in relief. "But you can't go and get yourself in trouble now either," I scolded him. "Or else I'll have to come out and save your ass." I gave him a little grin and poked him in the ribs with my elbow.

"God, what a relief." He dropped his head and smiled. "I'll be as careful as I can." He leaned down to give me a kiss. My hands automatically slid up his chest and around his neck. "Scout's honor. Now that that's settled," he said, sneaking a finger underneath my neckline, "let me see what's under that robe."

Darcy arrived at the cabin shortly thereafter. Remarkably quick, I thought, for having finished up at work and stopping somewhere to pick up a pair of Cole Haan hiking boots. "Listen, I'm not going to compromise on fashion just because I'll be hiking in the middle of a forest. After all," she said, looking down at them, "if I get a big story out of this, I'll just write them off."

I felt a little bit guilty that I'd already decided she and I were going to hang back. Hopefully she'd kept her receipt.

Fritz had taken up residence on the couch in front of the fire, feet up on the ottoman, laptop perched on his protruding belly. He looked like a very pregnant mother. "So, I've been thinking." He rubbed his beard thoughtfully. "We'll just start driving around to check these lots out." He pointed to the screen. "If anyone stops us, we're going to say we've been staying at the resort and loved the view so much, we wanted to build a cabin of our own on the same mountain. You know, like that other couple you mentioned seeing this morning." He set the laptop aside and slid on his boots, wincing in pain as he stood up. "Sure hope most of this is accessible by road," he said warily.

"To cover all the bases, I'm also going to head back down to the front desk and see if Caty happens to be in yet. I might mention that I know of a guy that's new to the region that deals in the hard stuff. See if I get any kind of reaction from her. Maybe she knows of him.

"But," he continued, "I really think checking out these properties and digging more into this Izzy dude is going to lead us to your dad. I've got a hunch they've got some kind of connection."

"Uh, I've got a slight change in plans." I stood there looking nervously between Fritz and Darcy, Michael's hands protectively on my shoulders. "I think Darcy and I need to hang back."

"What? No way!" Darcy exclaimed, spinning around, eyes wide.

"Please," I interrupted. "Just listen." I calmly explained my reasoning behind it, fibbing a little bit about just why we thought it was a good idea I stay behind too. (I wasn't going to tell Fritz that Michael didn't completely trust him.)

"I can come up with a disguise," Darcy blurted out. "Go undercover, incognito, or whatever. Dress me up like a dude. I don't care. I'm going."

I looked at her in her designer hiking boots, skinny jeans, stylish North Face coat, and flaming pink nails. She was a few inches taller than me with big boobs and long, beautiful, professionally styled hair. I was pretty sure she and I couldn't share clothes, and there's no way she'd be able to pass as a guy. Plus, I wasn't sure that she'd be able to contain her overeager self if they did find a big lead. If she was recognized, she might blow the whole thing.

"How about this," Michael spoke up. "Fritz and I go scouting around in our SUV to make sure everything's okay. Then if we give the all clear, you can come on up to join us." I noticed he didn't mention my name and wouldn't look me in the eye, but I let it go. He was just being overprotective.

Darcy looked seriously irritated, and I knew she was battling between her own desire to be in on the action, and the knowledge that, of all of us, she and I were the most likely to set off alarm bells. She sighed loudly, nostrils flaring and her breath coming out like a hiss.

"Fine," she spat out through gritted teeth. "But you check in hourly at the minimum." She paced around the room, shaking her arms in an attempt to dissipate her anger. "Why the hell did I spend $250 on these boots then?" she grumbled.

Michael and Fritz continued to get ready, packing food and drinks for their outing and discussing their cover story.

"Okay," Fritz began, "we say you're my son and we're going around looking for real estate deals in this beautiful area."

I looked at Fritz, who is about my height, and my husband, who towered over him.

"Yeah, I don't buy that. Unless your wife is an Amazon woman, you could not have produced that offspring."

Fritz glared at me. "I happen to have a brother who is quite tall." I titled my head at him in doubt. "Well, five-eight is considered tall in my family, at least. Anyway," he said, turning to Michael, "you wanna say we're a couple?"

"A couple of what?" Michael asked innocently, placing a bottle of water in a cooler. I covered my mouth to hide my snicker.

"A couple. As in, we're 'together.' You know, out looking for our forever home." Fritz looked completely earnest.

Michael stopped moving and turned around, his face beginning to turn red. "I'm on my freaking hon—" He stopped to take a deep breath, exhaling slowly. "No. We're not saying we're a couple." He began throwing the bottles of water in the cooler, ice splashing out.

"Aw, I'm just givin' you shit," Fritz laughed. "This one's so easy to rile up," he said to me, jerking his thumb back at my husband. Fritz's round belly shook as he laughed at Michael's discomfort. "We'll say I'm your father-in-law. You okay with that? That's a little more believable." Fritz winked at me.

"Fine by me," Michael agreed, slamming the cooler lid down. This was going to be a long day for him, poor guy. I could tell that much already.

"Okay, I think we're ready." Fritz slapped his hands together. He looked as if he were going to a party, whereas my husband looked like he was heading out for battle—face grim, dressed in a fitted black T-shirt and black jeans with hiking boots, the veins bulging out of his forearms. The only thing he was missing was an arsenal of weapons.

I walked up and put my arms around him. "Babe, you gonna be okay?"

"Yep," he said, stiffly. "You gals just hang out here until you hear from us." He gave me a firm kiss, grabbed the cooler, and he and Fritz walked out the door. Santa Clause and his bodyguard elf.

Darcy continued to pout about being left out of the search and kept her eyes glued to her laptop, claiming she was busy writing another story to air the next morning. I left her alone and went to walk down to the front office to see if Caty was around. We needed a little bit of separation to cool down.

The sky had begun to cloud over, and the smell of rain filled the air. I had forgotten to check the forecast and pulled out my cell phone to look up the weather. A light breeze played with my hair and leaves scattered across the path in front of me. Coverage wasn't great out here, and it took a few seconds for the app to pull up. Apparently, a cold front was coming through this afternoon, plummeting temps back into the thirties with a chance of freezing rain. Great. I was thankful the guys were in an SUV but decided to shoot them a text anyway to give them forewarning.

Wishing I had remembered to put my scarf on before I left, I continued walking to the main lodge. As I approached, I saw Caty getting dropped off by a big burly man in a Range Rover. He opened the door for her, and she stepped out of the back as he helped her down from its lofty height. The man was medium height and stocky, with the physique of a body builder. He looked around as if he was waiting for someone to jump out at him. Wow. Was that her boyfriend? Dude's got some cash to be driving that thing. Well, cash or a high credit line, which was more likely. The guy then went to park the vehicle and sat in it with it running, taking out his cell phone to keep himself occupied. He looked up at me as I walked by, a hard look on his face. I felt his gaze follow me all the way into the building.

Caty was quietly chatting with the guy behind the front desk when I walked in. From the way they were standing, it appeared as if she were giving him instructions. I studied her for a moment, letting them finish their conversation. She was very petite with long, dark brown hair, and her skin color looked as if she'd just recently been to the beach...or a tanning salon. She was probably on a first name basis with Darcy. I wondered if her job as resort concierge required fake tans and Botox. Highly doubtful, I hoped.

I was hoping to get her briefly away from the employee with whom she was talking, a guy named Fernando. I didn't really want to make my inquiries with any more witnesses than was absolutely necessary.

"Hey, Caty," I called out when they had a break in their conversation. I flashed her a bright smile.

Caty turned toward me, she and Fernando both perfectly attentive and ready to assist. At first, I wasn't sure she recognized me, as she studied me for a moment. Finally, she smiled. "Hello, Mrs. Drake."

"Are you working today?" I asked hopefully.

"Uh, yes. Yes, I am. I'm about to leave, but what can I do for you?" Didn't she just get here? Fernando gave her an odd look and she turned to him, dismissing him with a wave of her hand. "You can take a break, Fernando. I'll talk with you later." Maybe she was the manager? She was sure acting like his boss.

Fernando nodded and walked through a door behind the counter, disappearing and leaving me to talk to Caty freely.

"I have an odd question," I started. I was really feeling uncomfortable about this whole thing. I know nothing about drugs, drug lingo or any of that. I was the poster child of saying no to drugs. As in, my face was literally on a "Just Say No" poster in my school as a kid! I had never dabbled in drugs, nor had any desire to. But I realized maybe that would be to my advantage. Maybe I could simply act like someone who's interested in experimenting. Caty looked at me expectantly.

"So, someone thought you might be able to help me with something," I said quietly. I leaned against the counter and prayed silently that no one else would walk in.

"Okay, sure. What is it you need help with?" She folded her hands in front of her and tilted her head.

"I, uh, I'm...well...okay, I'll just blurt it out." I quickly peeked around to make sure no one else was within earshot. "I'm looking for some hooch," I whispered.

"Oh." She looked quite surprised. "Oh, okay."

I immediately felt myself blush. Even though it was legal in this state, I felt as if I were committing a major felony.

"You want the nearest location of a retail marijuana facility?"

"Yes, please," I immediately responded. But damn, I was supposed to be asking for something a little more hard core. I shifted from one foot to another. "Actually, uh, while that info would be great, um...I was hoping you could lead me to someone who could find me something a little more...potent? It's for a friend, actually," I added at the last moment.

She cocked her head at me as if she wasn't certain exactly what I was referring to.

"Oh, it's fine if you don't know a dealer," I quickly blurted out. I was beginning to feel bad. Maybe Caty just enjoyed a legal toke once in a while? Maybe Fritz's instincts had been wrong? "We can get by with the place you mentioned." Shame consumed me, and I resisted the urge to turn and run in embarrassment.

Caty looked me up and down, as if assessing my net worth...or maybe she was just trying to determine whether I was a cop.

"I swear I'm not wearing a wire," I said pathetically before mentally facepalming. God, she was never going to divulge anything to me now.

Instead, she tore a piece of paper off a resort tablet, taking special care to also remove the resort name from the scrap. She silently wrote a name and number down and handed it to me.

Still turning five shades of red, I thanked her. But I wasn't done yet. Fritz had wanted me to ask her if she knew of any new suppliers in town, hoping to gauge her knowledge of my dad and whether he was setting up shop in Elkston.

I looked at the scrap she had given me. "Soooo, this is the guy to talk to, huh?" I asked lightly. "My friend thought maybe someone else was honing in on his turf, what with the building downtown being blown up and everything."

"Huh. You know something about that?" she asked suspiciously. Her eyes narrowed.

"Nope. We just saw it on the news." My heart was beating out of control. What was I doing?!

"Really." She looked at me hard and I gulped.

I heard the bells on the front door jingle and turned around to see her burly boyfriend walking in.

"You 'bout ready to go, b—"

"Yep, just finishing up," she said, cutting him off.

She looked back at me and took a step closer, keeping her voice low. "This kid is the only source of anything in this town, and he has been for years." She pointed at the scrap of paper. "My advice is to be careful." I held her gaze, praying she couldn't see my heart pounding out of my chest. "Just be sure you don't get in over your head."

I gave her a nod and she walked around me and out the door. My legs nearly buckled underneath me and I leaned against the front counter in relief that the awkward encounter was over. She did not seem happy about being approached. I gave myself a few minutes to get composed before turning around to walk back outside. By that time, the sheet of paper in my hand was damp. Thankfully, this piece of paper hadn't started to turn to goo like another one before it.

I started to walk back toward the cabin, now more convinced than ever that Caty should not see Darcy with me. Caty had given me a dealer's name and knew I had seen the televised report. She knew I understood the significance of the explosion. She'd know something was up if she saw the two of us together. I didn't want her to think I was trying to get her in trouble, and I certainly didn't want Mr. Burly Man coming after us.

I looked down at the name on the piece of paper she'd given me. "Mo." That was it. The name Mo and a phone number. She'd said this "kid" was the only dealer in town and had been for years so, and assuming she was correct, he wasn't my dad.

As I continued my trek back to the cabin, I began to worry about Michael and Fritz. They had left to go drive around the mountain, searching for anything on the properties that might lead them to my dad. I think Fritz was convinced he'd come across my dad shacked up in a tent or in the massive mansion Izzy owned. I just hoped they'd be safe. The reality of what they were doing really began to set in. Driving around a drug lord's property uninvited was just asking for trouble. Would there be armed guards? I'd be surprised if there weren't. It didn't matter how built my husband was. A well-muscled, physically fit man is no match for a bullet. I had been foolish to think otherwise. A feeling of dread began to settle over me.

What were they getting themselves into? We didn't know much of anything about this Izzy guy, really. Why did he own so much property up here? Was he buying real estate as a way to funnel his drug money? Was he a drug dealer/entrepreneur? Omigod. Was that what my dad had done? Had he been buying real estate as a cover for his drug business? The thought of it made me crazy angry, and I kicked a rock in my path out of frustration, scaring a poor little ground squirrel, and in doing so, immediately felt ashamed.

The more I thought about it, the more I came to understand that my husband and my friend were risking their lives to find my dad. Why was I letting them do this? I was half tempted to call it off and go home to California. Did I really want to search for a person who obviously didn't want to be found? A person that had lied to me for possibly my entire life? A giant hypocrite who pretended to follow the letter of the law, but in reality, was probably a low-life drug smuggler? I sighed in frustration, feeling utterly defeated. Sitting down on a rock outside the cabin, I stared out at the valley below, whispering up a little prayer of protection for the ones I loved.

Darcy and I ate a light lunch. I had very little appetite, and she had packed all of the ingredients for a detox smoothie to make up for the muffin and restaurant lunch she'd eaten yesterday.

"You're killing me with these smoothies, Darcy. How often do you eat real food?" I couldn't help but make a face at all of the kale, celery, and grassy looking ingredients she was putting in the blender. "My gosh, how can you swallow that stuff?" I gagged just looking at it.

"This is what I have to do to make it in this business," she said with a serious face. Her behavior toward me had thawed a little bit after I came back from my adventure to see Caty, and she was no longer refusing to look at my face.

"I get it, but I think it's really unfair. You do too, or at least that's what you told me yesterday. You know your male counterparts aren't eating that for lunch."

"I know," she sighed, "but until I find some other career, I'm stuck drinking smoothies and getting Botox."

"Omigod, surely you really haven't had Botox. What are you? Twenty-seven? You don't have a single wrinkle on your body."

"It's never too early to start." She sounded as if she was quoting somebody else, and probably was.

"Fritz left his laptop here," she continued. "I pulled it out and booted it up. Can you believe that man doesn't have password protection?"

I laughed. "That does surprise me, since he's a PI. But frankly, I was shocked he has a laptop at all. I had always thought he'd be completely old school." I walked around the table to where she'd placed it. "I feel kind of bad snooping around his stuff while he's not here..."

"I don't," Darcy replied. "I'm going crazy sitting here, waiting for them to check in." She poured her smoothie and began to drink. My eyes got bigger and bigger as she chugged that thing down. When she was all done, her body gave a giant shudder and she put her hand to her mouth. "One minute," she whispered, finger over her lips. I could see her working to not gag it back up. "Okay," she said, exhaling. "All better. Now, where were we?"

We huddled around Fritz's screen. Darcy had pulled up several windows and began checking each one for updates. The microwave beeped as my leftovers finished heating, and I walked over to retrieve them.

Pulling my plate out, I nearly burned my hands. I set it down quickly and grabbed a fork while blowing on it to cool it down a bit. Darcy remained quiet and looked intently at something on the screen while chewing on her bottom lip.

"Holy..." she whispered. She glanced up at me quickly, then back down at the screen.

"What?" I asked. I opened a barbecue sauce packet and generously poured it over my pork.

"This is huge," she muttered quietly, furiously sliding her finger down the touchpad to scroll through something.

"What? What is huge?" I finished doctoring my plate and carried it back to the table, setting it down. "What did you find?"

She pointed to the screen, seemingly at a loss for words. Finally, she spoke. "Fritz's contact was able to get more of this stuff unredacted." She hesitated before continuing. "It's about your dad, Emily."

"What about him?" I didn't even know which window she was looking at, and I hurriedly scanned through what I saw in a futile attempt to understand.

"Your dad wasn't just *on* an FBI watch list, Emily." I looked at her in confusion as she pointed her finger to a paragraph in the still partially redacted document. My eyes followed, and what I saw shocked me. "Your dad *was* FBI."

•CHAPTER 19•

THE DOCUMENT WAS STARING ME IN THE FACE, taunting me. Hundreds of pages of intel were at our fingertips, and this was my first actual glimpse at them. My dad hadn't been a person of interest. He'd been an actual agent. Lisa and all of her crazy suppositions had been right. My dad had been a secret agent with the FBI.

We continued reading, sitting shoulder to shoulder, huddled over the screen. The room was eerily silent and my head began to pound. I had to remind myself to keep breathing. This wasn't the end of the world. This was actually way better than him being a drug smuggler, right? Then why didn't I feel any better?

God, had I put him in danger talking about him at the spa, right in front of the nail techs? They *had* been able to understand me. They'd keep quiet, wouldn't they? They wouldn't have any reason to retain that information, right? A part of me started to panic, wondering if they were really foreign spies. *Stop, Emily!* Two college-aged nail techs in a spa in the middle of the mountains aren't spies! Still, I couldn't stop my brain from coming up with endless what-ifs.

"Holy shit, I'm going to win an Emmy for this one," Darcy whispered to herself as she continued to read.

We brought the laptop to the couch and sat down side by side, kicking off our boots and stretching our legs out on the coffee table in front of the fire. A puff of eau de Fritz escaped the couch. I wondered when he had last showered.

There were still huge holes in the document, huge pieces of time blacked out. It was impossible to really understand what it all meant. We hurriedly scanned through what we could, so much of the terminology completely over my head.

From what I could tell, my dad had been an agent with the FBI since the late '80s. Ten years before his disappearance, he began working as part of a joint task force with the DEA, investigating drug cartels out of Mexico and Honduras. That explained all of the travel to Honduras and probably the phone calls to the cartel leader in Mexico.

But as I kept reading, the tone of things seemed to change. It appeared that the FBI had started becoming suspicious of some of my dad's movements. They started tracing bank deposits and followed his travel—even personal travel. They also put a wiretap on his phone.

I realized I didn't know how much of this was normal procedure, however. I would think that as any sort of government agent, you pretty much give up your right to privacy, knowing that you'll always be monitored for the safety of the country. But what if you're taking extra trips to Honduras that the FBI doesn't know about? Well, those trips possibly aren't "work related" and are a cause for concern. I saw words like "treason" and "possibly compromising the mission". I couldn't believe what I was reading.

It looked like the FBI thought my dad had become a dirty agent.

My pocket started buzzing and I jumped, knocking the laptop off kilter. Darcy saved it from crashing to the ground, and I pulled out my phone. It was a short text from Michael. *All's well. Nothing yet. Fritz is about to gas me out.* I laughed silently. Poor guy. It had only been a couple of hours. A few seconds later, he texted again. *Service getting spotty.* That wasn't surprising, as I'm sure they were driving in some pretty remote areas.

I put my phone away and focused my attention back on the laptop. This would take hours to sift through. I didn't know whether or not to bring it to Fritz's attention yet, since obviously, more information had been unredacted since he'd last laid eyes on it. I thought I'd better keep reading first since, after all, my dad's status seemed to change by the minute. *He's dead! Nope, he's alive! Wait, he was on an FBI watch list! Oops, he actually was FBI! Hold on, he might have been a dirty agent!*

Even though most of the document was blacked out, we managed to muddle through quite a bit. I wanted to skim through anything I didn't think was relevant, but Darcy was determined to read every last word.

"I'm a professional," she'd say when I'd try to page down before she was through reading. "I have to get all the facts, not just *some* of the facts. *All* of them."

Reading "all of the facts" was like reading a monotonous textbook of in-depth information pertaining to a subject you hardly know anything about. Lots of information about investigative procedures, joint operations with other US federal agencies as well as Mexican law enforcement, special investigative units assigned to work with certain cartels in an effort to take down rival cartels. How did one keep straight who was on the right side of the law? It was all baffling, like reading a Tom Clancy novel.

A couple more hours flew by as we read the documents, page by page. My mind was muddled by all the information in them, but I still didn't have any concrete answers. We soon realized we'd covered a lot of ground but hadn't again heard from the guys in quite a while.

"Michael did say reception was getting spotty," I said. I stood up to stretch out my legs and walk around the room. My vision was getting blurry from staring at the small screen for so long. I looked outside to see a bright red cardinal perched on the railing around the patio, staring in at me. It was a beautiful sight, the vibrantly colored bird in the foreground with dark green pines in the distance. The snow and ice made everything glitter and sparkle. Wait. Snow and ice?

"Oh, crap," I said, looking at the ground. "We've got at least two inches out there already." I turned around to look at Darcy. "I don't think Michael's ever driven on snow before."

"You should've thought about that before coming to Colorado in late September," Darcy scoffed, not the least bit concerned. Her eyes remained glued to the screen. "But don't worry. Two inches is nothing."

I rolled my eyes and turned to look back outside. The sky was gray and dusk was approaching. I could feel anxiety begin to wiggle its way into my brain. I tried to tell myself to calm down. They were, after all, two grown men...*neither of whom knows how to drive on snow and ice.* But they were in a 4WD SUV, which is great on snow *but slides like anything else on ice.* Surely, they were fine. They're resourceful...*but what if something's wrong and they can't get ahold of anyone because they don't have any reception?*

I took out my phone and sent Michael a text. *Everything ok? How r u handling the snow?* I tried to patiently wait for a response and distract myself by turning on the TV and watching an episode of *Fixer Upper*. I admit, I was distracted for about seven minutes until the commercial break. Then I started pacing, checking my phone every thirty seconds to make sure I had reception.

"Will you stop that?" Darcy finally said, setting the laptop down and stretching her legs out. "You're making *me* nervous."

"I just wish we'd hear from them." I looked outside as it continued to get dark. "Why didn't we set a time for them to be back? What if they plan to drive all night and I just don't know it? At what point do I start worrying?"

"Uh, I'd say you're already there." Darcy stood up and yawned, reaching her arms long while making a high-pitched screech. "Man, I'm exhausted." She looked at her watch. "And I need a change of scenery. Let's go get something to eat. My bedtime's approaching."

"But shouldn't we wait for them? What if they have news?"

Darcy waved her phone at me. "That's why we have these. They can call us once they're on their way back, and if we're not here, we'll still get the call." She shook her head in frustration, as if she were dealing with a child.

"Fine." I sighed heavily. I suppose she was hungry after only eating stringy green mush for lunch. I wondered if I could convince her to order a sixteen-ounce ribeye. Maybe I would order one for myself, just to spite her.

Darcy and I bundled up in our hats, coats, and scarves. No outdoor dining today. We both put our hiking boots on and stepped outside. The cold air hit us instantly, and I swear my nose hairs froze.

"You just want to drive over to the resort restaurant?" I asked, my nose already turning to ice. I had called the front desk before we left to make sure Caty had left for the day. I wasn't too keen on Darcy driving us all the way into town in this snow to eat.

"Heck no. We're walking. I've got to get some use out of these things." She held up her foot, her Cole Haan hiking boots already caked in snow. "Toughen up, California girl."

"Hey, I used to live in the Midwest. I can handle a good snowstorm." It had been about twenty years, but I wasn't going to tell her that. I took off on the trail at a brisk pace, slowing down as my feet began to slip on the layer of ice buried beneath the snow.

The path was nicely lit by the lamps, the layer of snow on them creating a peaceful halo effect. The wind was calm, and the falling snow made it look like a winter wonderland. Other than my nagging anxiety over Michael and Fritz, I almost felt relaxed by it all. We took our time walking on the icy path, taking in the sudden change of seasons. But soon enough, we were at the restaurant entrance, banging the snow off our boots and yanking off the coats and scarves.

Darcy and I enjoyed a nice dinner and got to know each other a little better. She ordered a real meal of blackened salmon with rice and mixed greens, while I chose a filet, baked potato, and creamed spinach. We each had a glass of the house cabernet, and with the first sip of wine, I felt my anxiety begin to abate. By the time dessert arrived (we split a piece of chocolate truffle cake), I was beginning to feel as if everything was going to be all right. The delicious dinner and decadent dessert, combined with the velvety smoothness of the wine, sated me. I sat back from the table, hands folded over my stomach, completely satisfied. It's funny how alcohol and good food can be so relaxing. It's as if all is right with the world. Looking back, I should have stayed right there in that moment for a while longer. Little did I know, in only a matter of hours, all hell would break loose.

• CHAPTER 20 •

AFTER OUR DELICIOUS DINNER AND DESSERT, we bundled back up and traipsed our way back to the cabin. The snow kept falling, and the weather app on my phone now predicted six inches. The path to the cabin had been swept fairly clean of snow and salted, and I was happy to see the area up to our front door had been completely cleared.

I unlocked the cabin door and we stepped inside to darkness. I swore I had left the light on just inside the door. I was certain of it. Something felt...off. I hesitated and looked around, my eyes easily acclimating to the dark inside. Darcy stopped behind me, sensing my unease.

"Uh, what's going on?" she said quietly. "Everything okay?"

I held up a hand to silence her. My eyes scanned the room. While my ears picked up the slight rustling of the few golden leaves still hanging from the trees outside, I heard nothing inside but the occasional pop of the cabin settling. Not willing to go any further in the dark, I flipped the switch, and the overhead light in the entryway came blazing on. I stood there, confused. I knew I had left that light on before we'd gone to dinner. I'd walked out last so I could lock the door. Had someone been in here?

Darcy stepped around me and headed inside to set her purse on the table. "Hey, thanks for dinner." She started ruffling through her papers, piling them into a neat stack. "I'm going to grab my things and head out. My bed is seriously calling my name."

I slowly took a step into the room and shut the door behind me. "Sure thing," I said, still unconvinced that everything was okay. "But will you stick around until I get this place cleared?"

She looked up at me in confusion. "Cleared?"

"I'm going to walk around and make sure no one else has been in here. It feels...off." Having lived alone for many years before marriage, I was quite used to that routine.

Darcy snorted, rolled her eyes, and continued to gather her things.

I grabbed the fireplace poker and, holding it like a baseball bat, began to methodically go through the cabin, looking under the couch and behind furniture, making sure no one was lurking. I couldn't put my finger on it, but something wasn't right. There was a slightly different, almost sweet scent in the air, and I felt very on edge.

I cleared the open family room and kitchen areas quickly, then moved into the bathroom, our bedroom, and closet. I even checked out on the back patio for footprints. Nothing seemed out of place, and no one jumped out at me from a dark corner.

I went back out to the living area and set the fireplace poker back in its spot. "Everything's okay," I said, though I didn't feel it. "I guess I'm just being paranoid." I crossed my arms and stood as if I were confident in my security measures, which I wasn't at all. I was really kind of creeped out. "Thanks for staying."

"Yeah," Darcy said, distracted. She looked around in confusion. "Have you seen the laptop? I thought I left it on the table before we left. Did you happen to pick it up and take it into the bedroom?"

"Which laptop?" I looked around, seeing Darcy's tucked nicely into her bag. "Fritz's?"

"Yeah." Darcy put her hands on her hips. "I know this sounds crazy, but I can't find it." She laughed, looking around the room. "I've looked all over. There aren't a whole lot of places to hide it here. I mean, it's not like I put it in a drawer." To be sure, we opened up all cabinets and drawers and looked under and among the cushions of the couch. Nothing. How does a laptop just disappear?

"You never took it into the bedroom, right?" I shook my head no. "We didn't take it with us to dinner. We didn't put it out in my car." Darcy crossed her arms over her chest and we looked at each other, a ripple of fear running through my belly. "I think you were right to be paranoid," Darcy said, a grim look now on her face. "Do you think we were robbed?"

We tore the cabin apart looking for Fritz's missing laptop. I searched where Darcy had searched, she searched where I had searched, and finally, we searched it again together, to no avail. I was right to think someone had been here. They'd been here and taken the laptop.

All of the information Fritz had on my dad was on that machine. Highly classified documents that he'd twisted arms and pulled favors to get had been sitting open on the screen when we left. I was kicking myself for being so stupid. Why didn't we lock it up? But then why would I have worried about a break-in at a high-end resort? And in the middle of a snowstorm!

Chills ran up and down my spine. I reached for my cell phone and called the front desk first, explaining what had happened (skipping over the "top secret" aspect to everything). Erik, the assistant manager, assured me that they'd immediately come right over to change the locks and assess the situation.

"Do you want me to stay awhile?" Darcy asked. "I'm wired now, and I don't think I'd get any sleep at home anyway after this. I feel responsible."

I hugged myself and shivered at the thought of someone else being in here, going through our stuff. "Yeah, if you don't mind." I leaned back on the kitchen counter, my mind reeling. "You're not any more responsible for this than I am. We should've locked it up, or kept it with us, or...something. But really, who on earth would have expected a break-in? Someone had to have known we had sensitive information in here. But how?" *Omigod,* I thought. *Had those nail techs been foreign spies after all?* No! That was a crazy idea! They were just college students. Nothing more. Right? Maybe this was just a random break-in and they got spooked and left before taking anything else. Still, I couldn't shake the fear that someone had overheard our conversation yesterday, and we'd lost Fritz's laptop—and so much intel on my dad—because of it.

Erik arrived at the cabin shortly thereafter, along with his handyman. He apologized profusely, citing this as the first break-in they'd had in the history of the resort's existence. (It was only three years old, but still.) He questioned me and Darcy at length, and we gave his as much information as we could without completely compromising the search for my dad.

In the meantime, the locks were changed, and the two men did another perimeter check of the property. Erik said all staff with access to the cabins would be questioned immediately, and he'd keep me updated. The police had been called, but due to the snowstorm and resulting accidents in town and on the roadways, they were unable to divert any resources tonight. They'd be out to question us in the morning, time and weather permitting.

Once the two guys were all done and we assured them we were fine, they left, telling us to leave all exterior lights on. I had a feeling I'd be sleeping with all lights on all over the cabin if I had my way. Of course, Fritz and Michael would be back any minute, and I knew I'd feel safer then.

I looked at my watch and was shocked to see how late it had gotten. "Crap, Darcy, it's already nine o'clock." Worried, I looked up at her. She had to be awake again in six hours. But more importantly, where were Michael and Fritz? "Okay, now I'm really beginning to worry," I said as I started pacing the room. "They've been gone almost twelve hours. It doesn't take that long to check out five properties, four of which are vacant of any buildings." When was the last time we'd heard from them? Around lunchtime? I knew service was spotty on that mountain, but we should have heard back from them by now. Michael would know I'd be worried. They should have *returned* by now.

I grabbed my cell phone and immediately called Michael. It went straight to voicemail. Same thing with Fritz's phone. I thought for a second and pulled up my FriendFinder app. Darcy walked over and joined me, our two heads together, staring at my phone, hoping for some answers. The app indicated his last location was on the mountain a few miles down the road from here. No surprise there. But that was at four o'clock, which meant they were still nowhere near here.

We looked at each other, our brows furrowed.

"They haven't called, they haven't texted, they've been out of cell tower range for five hours. Michael's phone would have pinged a tower at several different places on the main road back up here." I started chewing on my lip, trying to decide what we should do.

"Well," Darcy sighed, taking a step back toward the Keurig, "looks like we've got no other choice." She pulled out a coffee pod and put it in to brew. The smell of fresh coffee immediately permeated the air.

"What do you mean, 'we have no other choice?'" I rubbed my forehead as I tried to sort out the situation. We had to come up with a plan.

"Listen. Your husband and the old man are missing." I cringed, knowing Fritz would hate being called an old man. "They only brought along snacks, and they've been gone almost twelve hours, with no pings saying they ever went into town, and no pings since four o'clock.

"Someone broke into the cabin tonight and stole a laptop with some very incriminating information. Only that laptop. Nothing else is missing."

"Right," I nodded, agreeing with her. I knew in my heart of hearts that the burglar hadn't got spooked and left. They'd locked up on their way out. "It's like they knew what they were looking for. But how?"

"I don't know. But I think all of this is fishy, don't you? I don't want to stay here doing nothing, and I don't think you do either. We're going to look for them," she said resolutely.

"How are we going to do that? The police won't even come up the mountain tonight!"

"They won't come up because a B&E at a rich resort isn't high on their priority list tonight. They're not afraid of the snow, and neither am I." At my look of doubt, she continued. "I'm from Ohio, Emily. I learned how to drive on snow and ice. And I have a 4WD SUV. Stop worrying."

She turned around to pop another pod in the Keurig. This Cole Haan boot-wearing, Botoxed, spray-tanned, fake-boobed, brown-haired Barbie was going to drive us around a mountain in a snowstorm? *Well,* I thought, *if it might save my husband and Fritz? I'm in.*

• CHAPTER 21 •

DARCY AND I FOUND A FEW TRAVEL mugs in the kitchen and loaded them up with coffee—high-octane, fully caffeinated. I was surprised she didn't just grab a few pods to take with us to munch on. We also packed all the food we could find, with plans to get some more from the resort shop on our way out. I grabbed blankets, more layers of clothes, and some hand warmers that we'd brought along for the trip, and we loaded up the SUV.

I debated whether to tell the staff where we were going but wasn't sure whom I could trust. After all, one of them could be responsible for the break-in. Instead, I left a note on the kitchen table in the cabin. The police were supposed to be here in the morning, and in the event we weren't around...well, hopefully the right people would come looking for us.

Darcy went outside to warm up the car while I again pulled up Michael's latest FriendFinder location, entering it into my GPS. Not surprisingly, there was no direct route to that area. There were no paved roads leading the entire way there. We'd have to off-road, in the snow, in the dark, with only a GPS that may or may not work all the way there. To be safe, I downloaded the offline map to save us when we lost service. If only I could download an offline snowplow and team of Army Special Forces.

We hopped into the SUV and drove down to the resort's store. It was just before ten and I snuck in minutes before closing.

"Grabbing something for a late-night snack?" the staff person asked as she prepared to lock up for the night.

"Yep, something like that." I grabbed protein bars, bananas, water, and a bottle of whiskey. Don't they always give a shot of whiskey to people caught out in the cold in the movies? Well, it couldn't hurt.

I carefully ran back to the car and we took off at a snail's pace. The resort roads were slick, even with the salt and sand the staff had spread throughout the area.

Once we got to the main road, things started to get worse. The road hadn't been plowed or salted at all, and the snow kept falling. Darcy's SUV handled it well, the weight of it with a full tank of gas being enough to keep us from sliding off. We slowly began navigating down the mountain, following the main road according to the GPS. Compared to last night, we were crawling. Was it just last night that Michael and I had snuck off for our little rendezvous in the woods? He had sped around these winding roads without a second thought. So much had transpired in the past twenty-four hours. My gut tightened at the thought of Michael and Fritz being in danger. Would we be able to find them without endangering ourselves?

We crept down the mountain road. Snow flew at the windshield. The light from the headlights bounced off it and nearly blinded us. We saw no other traffic, and the road was eerily quiet. In the pitch dark, had it not been for the GPS, we would have had no idea how far we'd gone. Everything looked the same. I kept myself calm by thinking of how smart and resilient Michael was. He'd know to stay in the vehicle if they were stuck, right? And that neon green SUV would be easily spotted amid the snow. Besides, surely Fritz had done his share of work in cold climates. The two of them would figure out something if they were in trouble...I hoped. I wouldn't even let myself think of other alternatives.

Ninety minutes later, we'd gone two miles. Looking outside to see only darkness, snow, and the shadow of trees, I was completely lost. The GPS indicated Michael's last ping was a couple hundred feet east of our current location. But again, there were no mapped roads leading to it. Why had they gone this way? What had caught their attention that they decided to off-road?

We slowed to a crawl and I noticed a piece of metal barely sticking up out of a mound of snow on the side of the road. Could that be a clue or just a piece of roadside trash?

"Man, I shouldn't have had caffeinated coffee," Darcy moaned. She slowed the car even more. "I gotta pee."

"Well, see that piece of metal over there?" I pointed to the mound of snow.

"You want me to pee on a piece of metal?" she scoffed and looked at me incredulously.

"No. I want you to stop so I can see what it is. Maybe it's a road sign or something." I shook my head. "You can scout out a place to pee."

"Outside in the cold?"

"Where did you think you were going to go?"

"I don't know. I wasn't thinking ahead." She growled under her breath.

She pulled the car to a stop and hesitated. I opened my door and hopped out, my feet sinking at least six inches. "Are you going to get out?" I hollered above the now howling winds. She looked at me as if I were crazy. "No one is looking, I promise."

"Argh. Fine," she grunted. She grabbed some Kleenex, hopped out the other side, and crunched her way behind the vehicle to a small thicket of bushes. "Ouch," she said, tripping over something in the snow. She slowly crept behind the bushes and disappeared.

"Don't go far," I said. "People get lost easily in blizzards."

"How about I keep talking to you as I pee," she said sarcastically. "And besides, this isn't a full-on blizzard. It's just a snowstorm."

I couldn't remember there being much of a difference, but I wasn't going to argue.

While she took care of business, I walked over to the piece of metal, grabbing at it carefully with my gloved hand. It didn't budge. I tried again, but still nothing. *It must be frozen to the ground,* I thought. I started scooping away the snow surrounding it, jostling it back and forth at the same time. With one final yank, it came free, sending me back on my butt. Darcy walked up behind me.

"God, I feel so much better." She sighed in relief. "*Thank you* for making me get out of the car. Whoo!" She squatted down next to me in the snow and whispered, "Why are you on your ass? Did you figure out what that piece of metal was?"

I started to push myself up and dusted off my clothes. "Well, I was able to get it, but when I pulled it loose, I fell and it flew off somewhere. Look around." I hauled myself upright, grabbed my cell, and turned on the flashlight. Darcy did the same. We slowly swept the area with our tiny squares of light. The snow was coming down harder and I knew the metal would easily be covered up in seconds.

"I found it!" Darcy yelled from a few feet away. I tromped my way over to her. The piece was pretty bent, but otherwise in good shape. She turned it over as she wiped off the snow. "N—" She kept wiping, trying now to scrape at it with her gloved hands. "It's pretty iced over, but it does say something. Doesn't look like a typical road sign though. Go back to my car and grab the ice scraper."

I stumbled back to the car and searched around the front seat. Thankfully, I found it tucked in the glove compartment. It was small, but looked pretty sturdy. I hoped it could do the job. If not, we'd just have to bring the sign with us and defrost it in the car.

"Thank God," she said when I walked back over. She handed me the sign. "Here, I don't want to break a nail."

I propped the sign against my thigh and began to chisel away at the ice. Slowly, but surely, the ice began to break off. "N-O." Could this be the "No Trespassing" sign that Michael and I had driven past last night? Had they gone down that abandoned road? I kept scraping furiously, my breath fogging up the space in front of me. I was beginning to sweat from the effort. Finally, one last large chunk fell off, revealing the sign in its entirety. "No Trespassing." It was the sign from the abandoned mining road after all. And in the bottom right corner, which was slightly bent, was a small scraping of neon green paint.

Darcy and I looked at each other. The guys had gone down this road for sure, and apparently, in a hurry. Michael would not have cut the turn so close as to hit the sign without reason. Had they been chased down this road? In the pit of my stomach, I knew something was terribly wrong.

"This is an abandoned mining road. They went this way." I gestured to the barely visible clearing to our right.

"Are you sure?" Darcy asked. "How do you know anything about this road?"

Images of last night flooded my brain, and tears pricked my eyes. Last night in this very spot we'd nearly been hit by Dirk and Savannah barreling down this road. What was back there besides a nice secluded make-out spot? What the hell was going on? My hands started shaking as we headed back to the SUV. I'd been sweating a minute ago, but now I was shivering with cold and fear.

"I just do."

"Listen, everything's going to be all right," Darcy said as we got into the SUV and she started it up. "Okay? Don't freak out on me now."

"I'm not freaking out," I said, gazing straight ahead as she backed up and turned down the abandoned road. I set my jaw, blinked back my tears, and again pulled up the GPS. The app was now using the offline downloaded version. We now had no service because of the storm.

"Just take us down this road as far as you can. We'll go about 100 yards and then we're going to have to off-road."

"Whatever you say, boss." Darcy looked at me and shook her head, but followed my lead. Sure enough, just as I remembered, 100 yards in, the road seemed to end, and bushes and trees seemingly blocked the way. Their last ping had been just a little bit further.

We stared at our surroundings, barely visible in the darkness. "Turn on your bright lights and your fog lights. Anything possible that will help us see what's out here."

The area in front of us came ablaze as the SUV's bright lights lit up the snow surrounding us. We scanned from side to side. Where was the path? According to the GPS, we just had to keep going straight, but if we did that, we'd run straight into a grove of trees.

"Back up a little bit so we can see a bigger area."

Darcy complied and the SUV's tires began to spin. "Time to take it into 4WD," she said, pushing a button. Somehow the push of a button was anticlimactic compared to what I was expecting. The vehicle groaned and she downshifted, backing us up now with ease.

"There," I said, pointing to an area of broken limbs just to our right. "Could that be it?" Darcy eased the SUV over to the area, hesitant to go much further.

"Uh, I know you said off-roading was a possibility, but going through that mess is going to scratch the heck out of my car."

"I'll pay for any damages, I promise. Please, Darcy." I looked at her anxiously, my heart hammering and my voice constricting in my throat. "We might be running out of time."

She looked at the tree limbs one more time, sighed, and slowly accelerated. The vehicle bumped and groaned over the rough ground. Broken branches scraped loudly against the roof and doors.

Once we were through the trees, the vegetation cleared a bit, but the ground was still rutted and rough. The snow hid everything and we were jolted at every turn.

"Their last ping was just ahead according to the GPS," I said, pointing out into darkness. Darcy continued down the primitive road and when we hit a large rut, the SUV came to a shuddering halt.

"Great," she said and groaned in frustration. "We need to get out of this hole. Hold on." She rocked the vehicle forward and back, taking great care not to spin the tires. Finally, the tires caught and we lifted back up out of the hole.

"This should be about it," I said, unbuckling. "Let's get out and look around. I mean, I know they're probably not here, but this was their last known location."

I got out of the car and my breath caught in my throat. Snow swirled around me. Darcy was still inside the vehicle, digging around for something in the glove compartment.

"Ah, I knew it!" she hollered, hopping out of the SUV. "My little Maglite." She shook it at me, eyes glistening. "This thing may be tiny, but the amount of light it puts out is incredible. Plus," she said, sliding a finger through the key ring at the end and swinging it around, "it's pretty solid and can be used as a weapon."

"Great," I muttered. I turned on my cell phone's flashlight and shone it around. "Help me out and turn it on. See if you see anything." My little phone's flashlight, while good at any front door looking for a lock in the dark or under the bed to find dropped ChapStick, was not much use looking at the landscape in the middle of nowhere during a snowstorm.

Darcy fiddled with her Maglite, muttering to herself. "Now, why won't it...Come on now, really?" She tapped it on her hand and we continued to walk with the pitiful light from my phone and the vehicle's headlights shining before us. Once we got to the point where the headlights were almost of no use, we stopped. Frustrated, Darcy tossed the Maglite to me.

"I give up. You try."

I unscrewed the top, dumped out the batteries and put them back in in reverse order. The light clicked right on. Darcy was right. This thing was amazingly powerful. I shone it all around us, turning in a circle. A little bit ahead, the landscape seemed to slope, and the trees appeared much shorter.

"What's going on over there?" I said in wonder. We hesitantly walked further, brush tearing at our coats. Suddenly, the ground dropped away. I stumbled as my boot nearly slipped over the edge. My arm shot out protectively, hitting Darcy in the gut. "Whoa, stop!"

"Geez," she said, "watch yourself." And then she looked down, following the direction of the light. She gulped and took a step back. "Oh, uh, thanks for keeping me from walking off that cliff."

It wasn't really a cliff so much as a ten-foot drop. Just below, I could see what looked like another road. One that was cleared and free of vegetation.

"We have to figure out how to get down there," I said, shining the light around.

"Wait," Darcy said. She grabbed my arm. "Shine the light back to your right. I think I saw fence posts." I swung the light around until I saw what she saw and continued to follow those. Sure enough, if we turned around and headed back a little ways, we'd come across the connecting road.

I pocketed the Maglite, we returned to the SUV, and started it up. Ice had already begun to form on the windshield during our short expedition. We turned the defrost on full blast and waited a few minutes, warming back up ourselves.

"Do you need to pee again before we go?" I asked, half in jest, half completely serious.

"Very funny. Actually..." She thought a moment. "Nope. I'm good."

Darcy slowly maneuvered the SUV back the way we'd come and took a sharp right, driving through more brush until we entered a small clearing, and then drove onto a somewhat smoother path.

"Follow the fence lines. This is the road that connects us to the one we saw down below." My offline GPS map was blinking our location but didn't show any mapped roads anywhere nearby. "This must all be private."

"Even private roads are usually mapped," Darcy pointed out. "Someone is taking great pains to keep these roads hidden. Or more likely, Izzy has some government official in his pocket and is making sure the maps show only what he wants."

We rumbled slowly down the road, following the fence posts down the hill until we connected with the road below the ridge. That one was even smoother and wider, as if it were a full one-lane road, and Darcy was able to take the SUV out of 4WD.

"Do you think the guys made it all the way out here?" she asked, looking around. "I don't see anything. No signs of life at all. No tracks. Do you?"

The headlights shone bright against the swirling snow, and I was developing a severe case of vertigo. "I can barely even stand to look outside anymore," I answered, closing my eyes for a bit. I opened them up a few seconds later and let my eyes adjust to the contrast of dark and bright white.

"Wait a second," I said. My pulse quickened. Had I just seen a flash of light? Or was that my imagination? "Look up there. Way far ahead. Do you see a speck of light?" My eyes strained to look through the windshield. "Cut the headlights for a sec."

Darcy stopped the vehicle and cut the lights. Amid the blowing snow, a very dim light could be seen several hundred yards ahead.

"You think that's Izzy's house?" Darcy asked, squinting.

"Could be," I replied. "But if it is, we've got to think of how we're going to approach this." We sat in the dark for a few minutes, pondering what to do.

"Do you even think Michael and Fritz are really this far out? What if we're on a wild goose chase and their phones died and they went into town?" I knew I was grasping at straws, but I didn't know what else to do. "If we proceed, what's our game plan?"

"They've got to be out here," Darcy said. "Where else would they be? They—"

A sharp knock at my window startled us both, and we screamed in surprise. Turning to look out the window, I held up my hand to shield my eyes from the bright beam of light.

"What the...?" I muttered, my heart hammering. I automatically held up my hands in the classic surrender pose. We were trespassing, after all. But where did this person come from? A knock at Darcy's window told me he or she wasn't alone.

"Who are you? State your business!" a heavily accented male voice shouted at me. In haste, I decided to stick with the storyline we'd come up with earlier in the day. I rolled the window down just a touch, the cold air blasting through the crack.

"Hi! Sorry, we're out looking for my husband and father. They were driving around looking for real estate this morning before the storm came in, and they haven't come back. I was starting to get worried." Obviously, since I was out driving around in a freaking snowstorm in the middle of the night. These people were never going to buy this.

I struggled to block the beam of light intentionally pointed at my eyes. He was trying to blind me so I couldn't see him. The person on Darcy's side was doing the same thing. But then he moved his beam toward the back of the vehicle, looking for other passengers, I suppose. In that brief moment, I could barely make out the features of a very large horse with a rider. That's how they had snuck up on us. But how had they made it out here in pitch darkness?

"They're on horses," I muttered under my breath to Darcy. "How the hell did they find us?"

"Well, up until a minute ago, we had our lights on," she whispered back. "And horses have great night vision."

The men shone their lights back on our faces. "I think there are just two of them," I said quietly. "Can you hit the gas and outrun them?" I didn't want to hang around here any longer. I had a very bad feeling about all of this. We needed to head back to town and call the police.

"Well, I probably could," Darcy said, no longer whispering. "There's just one problem."

"What's that?"

"Yours has a gun."

• CHAPTER 22 •

THE ARMED HORSEMEN ACCOMPANIED us all the way to the main house, shouting at each other in a mixture of English and Spanish. Luckily, having lived in Texas and California and taken three years of Spanish in high school, I have a rudimentary grasp of the language.

"What are they saying?" Darcy hissed as she drove. She was indignant. "Don't they know who I am?"

"I'm pretty sure these two don't watch the morning news," I countered, looking at our captors. The horses were beautiful, deep brown quarter horses. Their breath streamed out their nostrils in giant clouds of vapor. The men on top of them were wielding large guns, but they were so bundled up I could barely make out any features. But the guns pretty much told me all I wanted to know. These weren't people to mess with. We were caught trespassing in the middle of the night on a drug lord's property. We were in deep trouble. Our only hope was that maybe Izzy didn't reside here. With any luck, we could play the poor, lost, helpless women card and maybe they'd let us go. Or sell us to the sex trade. I was hoping for the former.

"Can't you tell at all what they are saying?" Darcy kept pressing. "Why do they have to talk so fast?"

"It only seems fast because you can't understand a word they're saying." I was trying to concentrate and make out words through the cracked windows, and her yapping at me wasn't helping. "Be quiet for a second." I shook my head. Much of the conversation was muffled by the sound of the car and the thumping of the horse's hooves against the snow. "From what I can tell, they're going to lock us up with the others until they hear back from the boss."

"You think 'the others' are Fritz and Michael?" Darcy looked at me sharply.

"God, I hope so." I looked around as we parked and saw no sign of the neon green SUV. Maybe it was parked somewhere else? Maybe these banditos had intercepted Michael and Fritz at another location and brought them back here? More than likely it was hidden somewhere else on the vast property. I thought back to the footprint Fritz had brought up on the county assessor's website earlier. The place had looked palatial with several additional structures. The vehicle could be anywhere. The guys could be anywhere.

The men had us park near the front entrance and shouted at us to get out of the car. We did as instructed with our hands in the air.

The banditos hopped off their horses, and I was able to get a better look at them. One was tall and thin, with rugged skin and deep lines in his face, his cheeks red from the cold. He looked older, maybe in his sixties. The other was short and squat. He was much younger looking, with an angry face. Son or grandson, perhaps? Both wore cowboy hats, jeans and boots, with ear warmers, scarves and heavy coats to keep warm.

"Keys, keys," the old man shouted at Darcy. She tossed the key fob at him, her hands shaking.

"Crap, now I gotta pee again," she said, looking at me desperately, crossing her legs.

"*¡Cállate!*" the other yelled at her. Darcy jumped.

"She has to go to the bathroom," I explained. "Um, *el baño?*" I pointed to the two of us. By now, my own bladder was screaming as well, partly out of necessity, partly out of fear.

The two men looked at each other and shrugged.

"Marco, sácalos de mi cara." The shorter one waved at us as if we disgusted him and ordered the older one, apparently named Marco, to get us out of his face.

Marco herded us toward the front door, poking at our backs with the barrel of his gun. The entrance to this place was more luxurious than the one at the resort. This "home" was a two and a half story mansion with a wood and natural stone façade. Under any other circumstances, I would have oohed and aahed over it, but the constant nudging with the barrel of a gun kind of took my mood to a different place. The place was totally isolated and, despite our luxurious surroundings, I did not have a good feeling about this.

We entered the house, the foyer brightly lit, windows towering all around us. The floors were made of giant slabs of marble tile that looked as if they were flecked in gold. White walls stretched up nearly three stories to a large, ornate, circular skylight, currently covered in snow. Double staircases with wrought iron railings led up to the second floor. I slipped upon entering, my boots sliding easily on the shiny floor.

"*¡Ten cuidado!*" Marco hissed. *Be careful.*

"*Putas estúpidas,*" the shorter man cursed under his breath, still outside. His words weren't quite as...cautionary.

They herded us down the hall to a very large half bath, and Marco nudged us both inside, following closely.

"Excuse me! How about some privacy!" Darcy balked. She turned to face him, hands on her hips. Marco stumbled back a step. I grabbed Darcy's arm and dragged her inside the bathroom, shutting the door behind us.

"You cannot talk to them like that!" I hissed. "He's letting us use the bathroom! Just shut up and do what he says."

"Well, I don't have a clue *what* he's saying, exactly," she huffed. "I took two semesters of Spanish in college, and all I learned was how to ask for a beer.

"Now," she continued, glaring at me, "do you mind?" She flicked her hands at me, signaling that I needed to turn around. "Turn on some water, will you? I have a shy bladder."

I rolled my eyes, turned around, and turned on the sink water while she availed herself of the facilities. What was going to happen to us? I thought back to a self-defense class I had taken last year with one of my sorority girls. The instructor had started out by scaring us with real-world abduction statistics. "Never go with your captor to a secondary location," he had said. Then he quoted something like 90-95% of abducted women taken to a secondary location are either raped, murdered, or both. Well, we were already at our secondary location. Strike one against us. Now we might just have to fight like hell to survive. But first, we had to find Michael and Fritz.

Darcy flushed the toilet and I took my turn. She leaned her head against the far wall.

"Why didn't I just go home when I had the chance?" she moaned.

"Oh, thanks. So, you wish you had just left me?" I went to the sink to wash my hands, relishing the spray of warm water on my cold fingers.

"Well, yeah," she said and shrugged her shoulders like I was an idiot. "Of course I do."

"Listen," I whispered, keeping the faucet running to cover our voices. "We're going to get out of this." I could see her lower lip slightly begin to tremble. Through all of her badass investigative reporter machismo, I could tell she was scared. "We need to play the part of the dumb blonde, okay? We stick to our story. My hubby and dad were out looking for property and got lost. We came to try and find them. We know nothing beyond that."

"Right." She scoffed. "Like they're going to believe that. What do we say when they question why we're out so late?"

"We're still on West Coast time."

"And in this weather?"

"We thought it would be an adventure."

"What if they recognize me?"

"They won't." I hoped. Who watched the early morning news? Mostly people getting ready for an eight-to-five job or people just coming home from their shift. These guys didn't fit the news watching profile. "You stay quiet and let me do the talking. Got it? Just play along."

"I'll do my best." She sighed and didn't look too hopeful. Dark circles had formed under her eyes. Perhaps the long-lasting makeup was finally wearing off. She had been awake for close to twenty-four hours, I realized. She must have been exhausted.

Our armed guard was waiting for us when we left the bathroom, looking about ready to fall asleep himself. He grunted at us to continue with him and poked us in the back all the way up the stairs. One poke was a little too rough for Darcy, and she swung around at him, eyes flaring.

"Knock it off!" she growled. "El you-o estop-o! Capiche?" I cringed and waited for him to smack her across the face with the butt of the gun. To my surprise, he looked slightly chagrined and lowered the weapon across his body, jerking his head for us to continue.

Once we reached the second story, he walked us down a long hallway and opened a door, forcing us inside. I looked around to see a media room of sorts. Leather loungers were lined up, four rows deep, with a large screen at the end of the room. I was expecting more of a dark closet or a damp basement, but I guess when you're held captive in a mansion, crappy options are somewhat limited.

I turned around to see Marco eyeing Darcy. Crap. Did he recognize her?

"What is your name? Is it Marco?" I said to distract him. I didn't know how good his English was and wanted him to think we couldn't speak or understand much Spanish. Then maybe they'd loosen their tongues around me and I'd be able to interpret. Besides, aren't they always saying you should try to make friends with your captors? Or is that what you're not supposed to do? "My name is Emily, and this is...Abigail," I said, pointing to Darcy, who had already made herself comfortable in a lounger. Couldn't hurt to bluff her name.

The man turned angry and shook his head. "*Cállate,*" he hissed. He looked me up and down and quietly lowered his voice. "*Toma una pequeña siesta. Lo vas a necesitar. El jefe estará aquí muy pronto.*"

So far, I felt our conversation was going well. I had told him our names and he told me to shut up, go to sleep, and the boss would be in to see us later. Swell. Looking forward to it.

Marco left the room and slammed the door shut behind him. A soft click let me know he'd locked us in. I glanced back at Darcy to see she'd already passed out in a Barcalounger from exhaustion. Tiny snorts escaped her lips. I looked around the room and found a soft, fuzzy lap blanket to cover her up.

The room was pretty posh for an in-home media room. Besides the loungers and the screen, there was a concession area off to the side with an old-fashioned popcorn machine and soda fountain. Had I not been locked in this room against my will, I might have enjoyed it. There were no other doors and no windows, of course. I walked around and examined the air vents to see if, like in the movies, we could crawl out of them. Maybe if we were both the size of a cat...

I resigned myself to the fact that we might have to wait this one out. Maybe they'd let us go in the morning. After all, being "lost" on someone's property isn't a crime. Wishful thinking, I know.

Making myself comfy in my own lounger, I took off my coat and rifled through my pockets. I'd stuffed them with protein bars before we were forced out of the car, not knowing when we'd eat again. Taking one out, I ripped it open and took a generous bite. I'd try to stay awake while Darcy slept in case anyone decided to sneak in on us.

I shifted around in my seat, feeling along the edges for buttons or levers to explore any special features. Finding four buttons, I decided to try them out to see what would happen. I crossed my fingers and pressed one button. The seat began to vibrate slightly, and a slow heat emanated through the leather. Ooh, heated seats. Very nice. Button number two slowly reclined the lounger. This was *much* better. Button number three adjusted the headrest back and forth. This place was becoming far too comfortable. What would button number four do? Summon the butler? Smiling at the thought, I pushed button number four. Nothing happened as far as I could tell. I moved around, looking up and down the seat. No lights came on, no music, the movie didn't start playing. What did button number four do? *Had I really summoned someone*? That wouldn't be good. I sat up in a panic and looked around desperately to try to figure out what I had done. Scanning my head back and forth, I finally noticed the armrest between the two seats was slightly ajar. Maybe I had just opened that. I slowly crept my fingers to the edge of the armrest, nudging it open just a little bit more. Was there anything good inside? A key to the door, perhaps? That would be too good to be true. I glanced inside, seeing something dark and shiny deep down within. I reached my hand down and felt the cold, heavy metal against my palm. *Well, it's not a key,* I thought, smiling to myself. *But a gun will do just fine.*

• CHAPTER 23 •

I SLOWLY PULLED A RUGER LCP HANDGUN out of the armrest. My hand shook as I held it. I know nothing about guns (my astute observational skills allowed me to see the name was clearly etched on its side). Was the safety on? Where exactly was the safety? Was it loaded? I set it down gently in my lap and stared at it warily. On one hand, I didn't want it anywhere near me. On the other hand, I had somewhat leveled the playing field with this in my arsenal. Even though I didn't know how to use it properly or if it was even loaded, no one else knew that.

Darcy rustled around in her seat and burrowed farther under the blanket. I could wake her and see if she knew anything about handguns, but I decided to let her be. Right now, she was most likely dreaming of winning an Emmy and shooting to stardom, going from the morning news in Elkston, Colorado, straight to CNN. In her daily life, she'd normally be waking up shortly, getting ready for her early morning stint. Instead, men with guns had locked her in a drug lord's mansion, atop a mountain, in the middle of nowhere, with me.

I sat, still as a statue, the gun heavy on my lap. What would we do now? I couldn't just shoot my way out of here. We had to find Michael and Fritz before we could escape. But this property was enormous, and they could be anywhere. I had to somehow figure out a way to connect with them.

Amazingly, our armed guards hadn't searched us, leaving us with our cell phones. Short of tapping Morse code on the walls and hoping they were in the next room, I'd have to resort to my phone that probably didn't have coverage. I pulled it out hoping beyond hope that I'd be able to send a message to Michael. Maybe I'd get lucky and get reception just for one quick minute. I hastily typed in a text. *D&I locked in Izzy's house. Media room. Where r u?* I hit Send and watched the line scroll across the screen before stopping midway. I dropped my head and sighed. No go. As a desperate measure, I held the phone up to my chin and stuck one arm up, hoping to act as my own antennae. I held that position for at least a minute. My hand started to go numb. Finally, I heard a light swooping noise, signaling the text had gone through. I almost whooped with joy. Settling back into my seat, I held my phone against my heart and whispered up a small prayer that somewhere, somehow, Michael and Fritz would see that text.

Unfortunately, fatigue and the ridiculously comfortable seat I was in lulled me into a deep sleep. I'm not sure how long I slept, but I began to have an intensely real dream in which Fritz was a giant, his white bearded face larger than life staring down at me. His voice came out only as a whisper though, and I laughed at the dichotomy of the situation.

"Emily, wake up," he squeaked. I giggled to myself as his giant head hovered in the air above me. "Good God, have you gotten into the hooch too?" He tilted one side of his face toward me, giving me the stink eye. I sighed and snuggled deeper into my Barcalounger.

Suddenly, Michael's face appeared in the dream as well, his giant-sized arm swung around Fritz's shoulder. "Babe," Michael said, "see this guy right here?" His voice sounded odd, different somehow. He looked at Fritz, tears brimming at his eyelids. "This guy's my best friend." Michael wiped at his eyes. "I love you, man!"

This dream was funny. Michael would never say that in real life. I sleepily laughed to myself.

Fritz rolled his eyes and gently removed Michael's arm from around his shoulders.

"Emily, wake up, dammit! Your husband's higher than a kite and we need to get the hell outta here!" I shifted around, so comfy in my warm leather chair. I struggled to open my eyes, but I was paralyzed in the state between sleep and wakefulness. I knew it was all a dream and attempted to put the two of them out of my mind and slip even deeper into blissful sleep.

"Emily." An old, but familiar, voice entered the dream. Memories flooded my brain, my heart swelled, and I began to silently cry. My dad! That was my dad's voice! "Emily, this isn't a dream, honey. Baby, I love you and you need to wake up." I began sobbing now, as always happens when I dream of my parents.

"Emily," my dad said again. "Izzy's coming. You guys need to get out of here."

Izzy? Izzy? Who was Izzy? I sniffled as I tossed and turned, my mind stuck half asleep, half awake. Izzy...Izzy...drug lord...FBI...my dad...gun in my lap... Gun in my lap! I jerked awake and immediately sat up, my hand clamping down on the Ruger as it began to slide off my lap. My heart pounded as I grabbed the gun before it hit the floor. Omigod. If it had fallen, would it have fired a shot? My hands trembled and I blinked my eyes, remembering where we were. Darcy still snoozed quietly in her lounger nearby. What a crazy, crazy dream. I shook my head and breathed deeply, now fully awake.

Someone urgently whispered my name and my head shot up. Where was that coming from? Who was talking to me?

And then I saw them.

My dad and Fritz stared at me from the movie screen at the front of the room. *My dad* and Fritz? I shook my head and blinked again, unwilling to believe that I was really seeing him. I hastily wiped the tears from my eyes.

"Hey kid, thanks for joining us. I knew you'd come to our rescue." Fritz laughed, his head larger than life on the screen. "Guess what?" he said, looking at me expectantly. "I found your dad."

I choked back a sob and ran toward the screen, as if I could reach out and touch him. He was here! He was here? They had to be here somewhere, right? But how were they appearing on this movie screen? I pinched myself to make sure I wasn't still asleep.

"Hi, baby," my dad said, his face twisted in emotion. He reached out to me. "I can explain everything. I promise."

I struggled to hold back the flow of tears pricking my eyelids. My emotions battled in my head. Joy, anger, confusion, relief. But my heart won out and the elation at seeing him alive showed on my face. He sighed in relief, putting a hand to his heart.

Michael came onscreen and attempted to nudge Fritz aside. "I love you, babe," he said, making sloppy kissy faces. Then he got a huge goofy smile on his face. "See?" he said in amazement. "I met your dad!" He pounded my dad on the back, sending him lurching forward.

I gave Michael a thumbs up, still unable to speak, and shot a questioning look at Fritz.

"Five second run-down," Fritz said quickly. "I might've found some hooch in this room we're locked in and taken a few hits before leaving it to smolder right by your husband's head as he was napping." He gave me an embarrassed look. "Sorry. I did it purely for medicinal purposes." I raised an eyebrow at him. "You know, the sciatica?" He rubbed his beard thoughtfully as he continued. "Anyway, I didn't know Michael was so sensitive to the ganja."

Omigod, my husband was high. My jaw dropped and Michael giggled.

"But that aside, I'm going to get right down to it." His face turned serious, and my dad turned Michael around and walked him out of sight. "We got your text. We're locked in some room in this place, same as you. Your dad was able to hack into their wireless video intercom system, which is how we're talking to you." He gulped. "Hopefully we're only talking to you." He looked around the room. "I figure if no one has busted in here by now, you're the only room that can see us."

By this time, Darcy had begun to stir, sitting up and stretching out before stopping suddenly once she saw what was onscreen. I motioned at her to keep quiet, and we both listened intently.

"We're in some game room or something. Morons locked us in here with pool cues and darts and everything." He looked around again before pausing. "Not that they would do us much good as weapons with your husband in the condition he's in." I heard Michael singing Bon Jovi in the background. Fritz rolled his eyes. "Are you and Darcy okay?" I nodded and slowly lifted the Ruger. "Whoa, Nelly!" Fritz exclaimed. "Where the hell did you get that?" Darcy gave me a worried look.

"It was in the console," I said, finally finding my voice. I nodded toward the lounger. Darcy hastily opened the console by her chair and rifled through it, coming up with only candy wrappers and used napkins. She frowned.

"Is it loaded?" Fritz asked.

I shrugged my shoulders. "I have no idea. How do I even check that?" I flipped the gun over in my hands.

"Careful. There's no safety on that thing."

I almost dropped the gun right there and then. No safety? Seriously? I'd slept with that thing in my lap!

Fritz carefully walked me through how to tell if the gun was loaded and check how many bullets were left in the magazine. My hands shook and I felt nauseous as I followed his instructions, but he assured me the trigger wasn't sensitive. Most likely I wouldn't accidentally shoot my foot off. *Most likely.* That was reassuring.

"Whoa, babe! You got a gun?" Michael nudged his way back on screen. "Sexy!" He wiggled his eyebrows and my dad's hand appeared on his shoulder, dragging him out of view. Great impression my new hubby was making on my drug dealer/FBI double agent dad. I shook my head, thinking of the ridiculousness of it all.

"Okay, you should be good to go," Fritz said once he was finished going through *How to Handle a Handgun 101*. "Just tuck it in your waistband and use only when necessary." I did as instructed, pulling my baggy sweatshirt over it to hide the protrusion, and whispering up a prayer that he was right about the trigger.

"So, I assume you've met Marco and Diego?" Fritz asked.

"We didn't really have time for introductions," Darcy piped up, yawning. "Those two goons herded us inside with their giant semi-automatics and deposited us here." She glanced around the room. "Think there's any popcorn over there?" she asked me, nodding in the direction of the popcorn maker. "I'm starving."

I fished out a protein bar and tossed it to her.

"We came out here in search of you guys," I explained to Fritz. "Two guys found us outside and apparently weren't too happy with our presence. They forced us in here. I know Marco is the older one. Who's the kid? I assume they work for Izzy?"

"I'm pretty sure his name's Diego. But watch out for him. He's trouble." He rubbed his jaw carefully. Had Diego hit him? "I was able to pick up on a little of what they were saying, and Marco—"

"Polo!" Michael sang out in the background.

Fritz cursed, shook his head, and glared at Michael. "How the hell do you put up with this guy?"

"Well, he's not usually high," I said sardonically. My poor husband, the rule follower. He might never forgive Fritz for this one.

"Anyway, as I was saying," Fritz continued, "Marco said something about *el jefe* coming in to talk to us later. You know, *the boss.* That's got to be Izzy."

My dad edged his way back onscreen. "You should never have come here, Emily. You've got to get out of here before Izzy gets back." His eyes widened in concern, and he ran his hand down his face.

"I can't believe I'm talking to you, Dad." His face fell and he looked ashamed. I closed my eyes and started over. After all, his explanations could wait. We had more pressing issues to address. "We all need to get out of here," I agreed. "How—"

"No. I'm staying," he said with determination. "I'm staying, but you need to go. You've got to trust me on this."

Trust him? He'd lied to me for my entire life, let me believe he was dead, and now he was telling me to trust him?

I shook it off and spoke up. "If we're going anywhere, you're coming with us." Anger and frustration began to wriggle their way into my body, and I could feel my face getting red. We didn't all drive up here, risking our lives in the middle of a snowstorm to go back empty-handed. After all, the end game was finding my dad. Now we'd found him, and I was not leaving without him. Besides, why the hell would he want to stay? Wait. Was he hoping to finalize another "business transaction"? The thought of it made my blood boil.

"You trying to score another drug deal, Dad?" I hissed, unable to hold back any longer. "Can't leave that part of your deceitful past behind you?"

"Oh boy, Emily's pissed," I heard Michael whisper loudly off-screen.

"Haven't you caused enough trouble and heartache?" I felt my face flush with anger, and the words continued to spill out of me. "You lied to me and mom for all those years." My dad's face turned to stone. "I know everything, Dad. *Everything.*" Well, really not everything. I hadn't finished reading the entire FBI file before the laptop was stolen. But I'd read enough.

"Emily, I can—"

"Yeah, you'd better explain. You'd better explain how you can live with yourself after what you've done. Are you a double agent, Dad? Have you turned against your own family and your country to be on a Mexican drug lord's payroll? And for what?" I raised my hands in helpless confusion. "Fame and fortune?" I sighed, shaking my head. "Did you fake your own death?" I stared him in the eyes, willing him to come clean. Instead, I was met with silence.

"And what about Mom?" His stony veneer cracked, and I could see his eyes well up as he dropped his gaze to the floor.

"Your mother is dead, Emily," he said quietly, in defeat. "She died in the accident. That is the truth."

I wrapped my arms around myself, squeezing hard as sobs escaped me. I'd known this for almost two years, but finding out my dad was still alive had given me a glimmer of hope.

"And that's why I can't leave here," he continued. I took a deep breath and looked up at him. His jaw was set and his eyes darkened. "This family put a hit on me and your mom. She died, and I barely escaped with my life." I sniffed and wiped the tears from my eyes. Darcy walked up and put her arm around me, squeezing my shoulder in support. My dad looked me straight in the eyes, all emotion disappearing, and his face again turning to stone. "And *I'm* not leaving this place until Izzy is dead."

• CHAPTER 24 •

"LISTEN," FRITZ INTERRUPTED, "the goons don't know George is here." I furrowed my brows in confusion. "It's a long and complicated story."

"I'm not going anywhere," I said, my crossing my arms. "And why don't you go ahead and explain how you two came to be here?"

Fritz looked at my dad and sighed heavily. "Michael and I may have parked the SUV down the mountain and hiked up here to snoop around. We may have invited ourselves inside and gotten caught."

"May have?"

"Well, what the hell else were we supposed to do? That thing is bright neon green! You can see it for miles!"

"What happened to the plan? Driving around, pretending you were looking at real estate?"

He shook his head and shrugged his shoulders. "Yeah, I never thought much of that plan. I only came up with the idea so you'd stop worrying."

My jaw clenched. "So, instead, your brilliant idea was to snoop around and get busted."

"It got us inside, didn't it?"

"Knocking might have resulted in the same thing."

"Yeah, well—"

"Forget about that," my dad interrupted. "It doesn't matter how they got here. What matters is that you get out before Izzy gets here. You are not safe here. None of us are."

"Well, just exactly how do we get out of here?" I leveled my gaze at him. "And how are you locked up with Michael and Fritz without anyone else knowing you're here?"

"I've been around this area for a couple of days, ever since the explosion, waiting for Izzy to show," he grumbled. Darcy elbowed me in the ribs and I growled under my breath at her in return. "I hid out in the stables with the horses, broke into the basement of the house, snuck around to steal food. It hadn't been too hard until these two showed up today." He jerked his head toward Michael and Fritz.

"And how did you come to be in the same room with them if you've been sneaking around the property unnoticed?"

Fritz gave my dad a wry look.

"Well, um, that's an interesting story," my dad said, looking down.

Michael stumbled into the background and suddenly looked up. "Oh yeah!" he said. "This dude tried to kill me earlier!" My eyes opened wide. "Man," Michael said, shaking his head and sounding forlorn, "and he's my father-in-law!"

I heard Fritz shushing Michael and telling him to sit down and rest.

"You tried to kill my husband?" I hissed. Seriously? Could this get any worse?

"Well, to be fair, I didn't recognize him," my dad said sheepishly. "I was hiding out in this room when the goons brought them in. I didn't know who they were at first, but I knew I had to get the heck out without being noticed. So, when he sat on the couch, I snuck up and put him in a sleeper choke hold—"

"A sleeper choke hold? So, wait a second. He wasn't 'napping' earlier, was he? He was unconscious!"

My dad shrugged his shoulders.

"And where were you while my husband was in a choke hold?" I directed at Fritz.

"Well," he cleared his throat, "upon being forced into this room, I may have begun searching it. I may have come across a nice stash of MaryJane and perhaps was looking for a light at the time your dad, uh, did that." He held his hands up and shook his head, like he just couldn't help it.

Darcy snorted.

"Omigod. So, you're telling me that while you were busy lighting up a joint, my dad was trying to kill my husband." My dad and Fritz looked abashed, while Michael heaved loud, heavy sobs in the background.

I felt like I was on a reality TV show. Was this really my honeymoon? I looked at Darcy and clenched my teeth. We'd been locked up by people with guns on a drug lord's property after chasing after my "presumed dead", possible FBI double agent dad, who had put my husband in a choke hold while my oblivious hired private investigator was getting high to relieve pain from his sciatica. Despite the seriousness of our situation, a giggle escaped my lips. Darcy looked at me, pressing her lips together, also trying to muffle a laugh. However, neither of us could contain ourselves, and we soon both exploded in laughter, tears running down our cheeks. Fritz looked at my dad, and soon they too were laughing. Michael wedged his way in between the two of them, his tear stained face red from crying.

"Babe," he hiccupped, "you okay?" His mouth hung open and his eyes looked glazed as he stared into the screen.

I nodded my head and doubled over in laughter.

"My head hurts," he said, sighing heavily as he turned around to walk off.

The laughter eventually died down and, sadly, we were again faced with the seriousness of the situation. Darcy went to the soda machine and filled up two glasses, returning to give me one.

"Wait, something doesn't make sense here," she said. She slowly stirred her drink with a straw. "Mr. P., how didn't you recognize Michael today when you saw him last weekend at the wedding?"

"I wasn't at the wedding," my dad replied. He shook his head and looked at me. "I knew all about it, hon, and I'm sorry. But I'd never put you in that kind of danger. What's she talking about?"

"Someone left me a note, and they signed your name." I explained the note to my dad, and how it had turned to goo once it hit the water, and Fritz's resulting lab analysis.

"Who gave the priest that note? What did he look like?" he asked, puzzled.

"Well, apparently he was a tall, white male with dark hair. Mid-thirties, pretty muscular, with some body ink," Fritz said. He walked off-screen for a moment and I could see Michael passed out on the pool table. Loud snores escaped his mouth.

"Hmmm," my dad said quietly, furrowing his brow in concentration. "There is one person I can think of that fits that description, but..."

"Who?" I asked when his voice trailed off. "Who was it?" I wanted to know who'd followed me to California. Who knew so much about me, and apparently my dad, that they'd show up at my wedding and risk being seen, only to leave a forged note? It didn't make any sense.

"No one you'd know," he replied. He leaned back against the pool table behind him, Michael oblivious to the company.

There was so much about my dad that I didn't know. So many questions I had. I only hoped we'd both live to see the day when I could get those questions answered.

I walked over to the soda fountain to refill my drink. Grabbing some peanut M&Ms off the counter, I made my way back over to the screen.

"So, what's your big plan to get us out of here, Mr. P? Oh, and Darcy Jensen of KVKX by the way." She tipped a finger to her forehead in a mock salute. My dad nodded in return.

"I haven't thought of that yet," he replied. He closed his eyes and rubbed his forehead. I still couldn't believe he was alive and that we were in this miserable situation. All I wanted to do was go to him and hug him. But reality dictated otherwise.

"Well, we can't really go anywhere until this lug wakes up," Fritz said, jerking his thumb at Michael. "And when he does, I have a feeling he's gonna be a force to be reckoned with. Actually," he continued, "I'd kinda not like to be around for that." He looked around at the exits.

"Don't you dare leave my husband behind," I warned him. "You're the reason he's in this condition." I gave Fritz my sternest glare and he chuckled.

"Oh, Emily. I'm not going to leave this guy behind, trust me. Plus, if I could get out, I would've already," he muttered.

"And no more joints."

He raised his hands in defeat and walked away.

My dad sat there, pondering what to do next. After several minutes of silence, he spoke, his tone grave; it was the voice he used only when I was in serious trouble as a child.

"I'm going to come break you out. I've got to get you out of here before Izzy gets here. We can't wait any longer."

"You're coming with us, Dad," I countered.

He looked up at me, his face set with determination. "I already told you. I will come down this mountain when Izzy is dead."

"But Dad, I think the best idea might be to—"

Suddenly, I heard a scratching at the door. Darcy's head shot up, her eyes frantic. She slashed a finger across her throat and I hissed at my dad, "They're here! They're here! Cut us off!" I heard a small click and the door began to swing open. My breath caught in my throat and I willed the screen to go black, my hands shaking in fright. Darcy grabbed our cups and threw them in a trash can like a teenager about to get caught drinking, while I stuffed the peanut M&Ms in my pocket. She threw herself into a Barcalounger and pretended to be asleep. Just as the door swung wide, the screen blessedly went black. A huge breath escaped from me, and I thought I'd pass out from relief.

"What are you doing in here, *mis chicas gringas*?" The shorter man, Diego, entered. The Ruger sat comfortably in my waistband, but that knowledge gave me only a smidge of confidence. Most likely, I'd use it to hit someone over the head before I'd shoot them with it. But again, he didn't know that. Diego gave me the creeps, and I was sure I could be persuaded to pull the trigger if I had to.

Darcy opened her eyes at the sound of his voice, stood up, and edged closer to me. She took my hand to stop the trembling. "What do you want?" she said slowly, in a loud voice. "Remember, I no-espeako-de Espanol."

"Stupid bitches," he muttered, shaking his head, a sneer on his face. "You understand that?"

I had known what he and Marco were saying all along. And most of it wasn't nice. But I stayed quiet, still pretending I didn't know any Spanish.

"Listen, why are you holding us here?" Darcy asked. "We haven't done anything wrong." She looked at me and continued. "And, uh, my friend here needs her medicine. She's diabetic, and she could go into a coma."

Oh, boy, I thought, *she's using the oldest line in the book.* I thought of the two cups of soda I'd had and the peanut M&Ms in my pocket. I hoped Diego wouldn't look in the trash can.

"*Mierda,*" he said. *Bullshit.* "You no look sick."

Darcy nudged me none too gently. "Play the part," she whispered. I staggered to the side at her jab, feigning light-headedness.

"Hmmm," Diego said, rubbing the spotty goatee on his greasy face. Why do some men insist on growing facial hair when they so obviously shouldn't? A spotty goatee doesn't make you look like a man. It makes you look juvenile. The large semiautomatic, however...well, that makes you look like a crazy juvenile.

"Izzy no like this. You no get sick on Izzy's floor." He glared at me, held up his gun, and retreated, shutting the door and taking care to lock us in once again.

We both exhaled in relief when he was gone.

"Maybe that bought us some time," Darcy said.

"Or maybe they're going to check on us more often, now that they think I'm 'sick.' Why did you even say that?"

"I don't know." She started pacing back and forth. "That's what reporters are taught to say whenever we're covering a story about a missing child. You know," she looked at me pleadingly, "to try to convince the kidnappers to release them."

I heaved myself back into a lounge chair. "Yeah, well, I'd say most kidnappers have no compassion, and neither do these guys."

"Well, they did let us pee."

I rolled my eyes and thought a second.

Marco did. And he had looked a tad bit remorseful when Darcy had yelled at him for prodding her with the gun. Out of the two of them, he was the most compassionate. He was definitely the one we'd have to work on to get him to help us if we wanted to get out of there alive. But how?

• CHAPTER 25 •

DARCY RESUMED HER LOUNGING POSITION, and I paced in the media room, anxious to hear back from the guys.

"We have to find a way to get out of here," I said, arms crossed. I chewed on my bottom lip and gazed around the room. There was only one exit. No windows, not even a bathroom. That seemed odd to me. You'd think there would be all kinds of escape routes available in a drug lord's house. Tunnels, even. I thought some more, looking around the room. Maybe there were. Maybe they were just hidden.

I started gently knocking on the wall, moving up and down, pressing my ear flat against it in an attempt to listen carefully for any change in pitch.

"What the heck are you doing?" Darcy asked, disdainfully. I shushed her, and after a minute, she stood up to join me.

"There's got to be a secret passage out of here, don't you think? I mean, Izzy's a freaking drug lord, for goodness' sake. Surely, he has more than one exit from a windowless room. I'm trying to find it." I kept tapping up and down the wall, listening for a subtle change in sound. Of course, I had no idea what kind of sound I was supposed to hear. A hollow sound? An echo? Someone on the other side telling me to knock it off (no pun intended...okay, pun intended.)

Darcy sighed. "Someone has played one too many games of Clue," she mused. "If we find one, do you think it will lead us to the study or the conservatory?" I chose to ignore her. She shrugged her shoulders and begrudgingly joined me. Together we gently tapped on all four walls in the room, taking our time. After about twenty minutes, we'd gotten nowhere. I began to doubt my theory.

"There's got to be another way out of here," I growled. I walked up to the huge screen, which was really nine individual screens meshed together as one big screen. Looking behind them, I saw nothing but cords, holes, and mounting units. A large red power button on the side of the bottom right screen stared me in the face as I pressed my head against the wall and struggled to see a hidden lever that wasn't there. What was I hoping for? A flashing light and a big red arrow?

"What next, Sherlock?" Darcy said sarcastically. She lifted her arms in frustration. "Well, if nothing else, the station will notice I'm missing when I don't show up for work in...oh...thirty minutes." She leaned back against the wall behind me and closed her eyes.

"Right," I said half-heartedly. I wasn't going to give up and wait to be rescued. We had to get out of here sooner rather than later. Of that, I was sure. There had to be some other way out of this room. We were so close, I just knew it. I rested my head against the wall, letting my vision blur for just a second. The big red power button swam in and out of focus. Wait a second. Would that just turn on the screens or did it serve some other purpose? Could that possibly be the key to our escape? I reached up tentatively and pressed the button. Holding my breath, I waited for something to happen.

Nothing.

Frustrated, I banged my fist against it, not really caring if the whole place heard us. We had to take action. We had to get—suddenly, the wall started to shake. I froze and turned my gaze slowly.

"Whoa!" Darcy chirped. Her arms flailed as she struggled to keep her balance. She stumbled back as the wall behind her gave way, her body falling into darkness. I whipped around and tried to grab her arm before she hit the ground, but my boot caught on the lip of the floor, and we both tumbled to the ground. The wall then closed up behind us and we were swallowed up by darkness.

"Nooooo!" Darcy said. "I need light. I need light! I'm claustrophobic!" Her voice began to rise in panic, and she started to squirm, putting a death grip on my arm. I grabbed my phone to turn on the flashlight.

"Breathe," I told her. "Breathe. Everything's going to be all right." Overhead, lights started to flash, and I could see small fluorescent bulbs slowly flickering to life. A dim glow began to light up the space, and Darcy's grip on my arm relaxed just a bit.

"This is unbelievable," I said, my voice just a whisper. I pushed myself up to standing and looked around. We were in a small, enclosed hallway of sorts. It was no more than two feet wide and windowless. A musty smell filled the air, and I knew Darcy wouldn't be able to keep her claustrophobia at bay for long in here. The passageway was long with randomly placed doors on either side. I figured it must run the length of the house. The doors must open to each room that had access to it.

Turning around, I desperately grabbed the doorknob that led to the media room. It was locked. What kind of secret passageway lets you in but has no way back out? Chills crept down my spine, and I began to feel a bit claustrophobic as well. I bolted to the next door and tried the knob. Nothing.

Had we triggered some kind of alarm when we escaped our room? Was the house fully locked down? Would they come looking for us? They'd have to know where we'd gone. Besides the door to the hall, which had been, presumably, guarded, this passageway was the only way out.

Our only option was to continue moving until we found the exit. I just hoped we could find it before the banditos or Izzy found us.

"Emily," Darcy said, her voice breaking as she fought to hold back tears. "I gotta get out of here." Her eyes darted back and forth around our small, enclosed space. "I can't do this." Her breathing quickly became shallow and rapid. I grabbed hold of her hand and she squeezed mine so hard I thought my fingers would break. "I really, really can't do this. We're trapped in here!"

"Hey," I said, wresting my hand from her grip and putting both hands on her shoulders, "we're going to get out of here." I pointed down the passageway and kept talking. "Like in every good mystery game, there's an end to this secret passage." I gave her what I hoped was an encouraging smile. "We just have to find it." Grabbing her hand, I began to pull her down the hallway. "One of these rooms has the guys in it, right?" They could be in the basement for all I knew, but I was trying to think positive.

"I guess," she said quietly.

"Then we need to figure out which one it is. Pay close attention to anything you hear." We tiptoed to the next door and pressed our ears against it. I could only hear my shallow breathing and looked up at Darcy to make sure she wasn't holding her breath. The last thing I needed was for her to pass out on me.

"Nothing," she whispered. Her eyes darted to the next door and we hurried down the hall.

We both put our ears to the door and I held my breath. I could feel a subtle, intermittent vibration against my cheek. What *was* that? Tilting my head a bit, I pressed my ear harder against the door. The quiet, rumbling noise faded, only to come back a second later. It was quite rhythmic...almost like breathing. Was that Michael snoring?

My eyes darted up to Darcy's, and she nodded, indicating she'd heard it too. We waited a beat, quiet as mice. My breathing was so shallow, I was amazed I didn't pass out then and there.

Suddenly, I heard mumbling from the other side of the wall. Could that be Fritz or my dad talking? Darcy and I both strained to hear, our foreheads touching. Darcy whipped her head up, jacking my forehead in the process, and gave me a big thumbs up.

"It's them! It's them!" she whispered excitedly.

"How do you know?" I asked, rubbing the sore spot on my head. I hadn't been able to make out anything discernable. For all I knew, Izzy could have been in there, and I didn't know what Izzy sounded like at all.

Darcy looked at me like I was crazy. "Don't you recognize Fritz's voice?" I frowned and shook my head no.

"Well, you are older, and the range that older folks can hear decreases with every passing year." She nodded her head like she'd just explained one of the secrets of the world. As if I can't hear as well because I'm a full—what—five or so years older than she is? Whatever. I rolled my eyes and sighed.

"Are you sure it's them?" I asked. How would we get their attention? We'd have to make some kind of noise for them to notice us so they could open the door to the secret passage. If we were wrong about who was in that room...well, I wasn't going to think about that.

"Yes. I'd stake my life on it." Darcy looked completely serious, and I hoped she wasn't only set on getting out of this passage to relieve her claustrophobia. If she was wrong about who was in that room, we were dead.

I hesitated a brief moment, then slowly began tapping on the wall. My dad had taught me Morse code when I was little, and we used to tap to each other from different rooms. Funny, I'd always thought it was just a game. I had no idea he probably used it on a regular basis, and I'd have a need for it in real life down the road. Would he remember our special code and be able to decipher it?

I tapped out "DAD" using softer, quicker taps for the dots, harder taps for the dashes. I paused for five seconds when I was finished, and then began again. The room on the other side of the wall became silent but for Michael's rhythmic snoring. Either they couldn't hear me, were listening intently and silently, or had visitors. Or we had the wrong room altogether. Dare I knock any louder?

After tapping through his name twice, I paused again, held my breath, and counted to five. Immediately, distinct tapping could be heard coming from their side of the wall. Darcy and I both jumped for joy, muffling the taps entirely.

We quieted down and pressed our ears against the wall. Silence. *Oh please, God,* I thought, *let them try again.* Then I heard it. One soft tap, followed by two harder taps. "EM". He was communicating with me! He remembered!

Relief filled my body as I shakily began to tap out abbreviated instructions for them to look for a red button to open the wall. My dad was an FBI secret agent. Surely, he'd be able to figure this out, right?

We waited patiently as my dad and I communicated back and forth. The passage was becoming warm from our excitement, and I started to sweat. I feared Darcy's claustrophobia would become worse the closer we were to breaking out. Minutes passed with no sound. Were they scouring the room for the red button? Was their opening to the passage different than it had been in the media room? Or had Marco and Diego come back for them?

Darcy slid down to the floor and closed her eyes, breathing deeply. Her lips moved as if in prayer, and she looked to be in a meditative state. Sweat trickled down my chest and I lifted my hair from my shoulders in an attempt to cool off. I glanced up and down the passage, wondering if we should try another room instead. Surely one of the doors opened from this side. What kind of moron builds a passageway you can't get out of? There had to be an exit somewhere. I felt like we were running out of time. I reached up to tap out another message to my dad, hoping they were still in there, and I wasn't about to give us away to the bad guys. Just as I began to tap, the door slowly swung open. I nearly collapsed in relief.

• CHAPTER 26 •

DARCY SPRANG UP AND RAN INTO THE ROOM, straight into my dad's arms. Though we'd only been in that cramped, musty passageway for minutes, it had felt like much longer. Her relief was palpable, and she sobbed in gratitude. Fritz had a big smile on his face. I looked over to see my sweet husband still passed out on the pool table. He'd slept through it all.

Darcy stifled her sobs and stepped back from my dad, allowing him to get a good look at me. I couldn't move and remained rooted to my spot. We hadn't seen each other in person for nearly two years. In spite of the fact that he may have been a drug runner and a double agent, (I still couldn't reconcile that in my brain.), he was still my dad, and my heart ached.

I looked him over and couldn't believe how much he'd changed. Thinner than I remembered, his hair had grayed considerably and now curled over the tips of his ears. Wrinkles that had been evident before were now much more pronounced. The past two years had aged his face at least ten. I wondered if he thought the same of me.

He opened his arms to me and beckoned me to him, a questioning look in his eyes. My brain hesitated, but my heart won out and, finally able to move, I rushed to him. He wrapped me in his arms and held me close.

"I can't believe you're here," I choked out repeatedly. We gently rocked back and forth and I took in the scent of him. Everything felt so surreal. I felt like I was hugging a ghost. My heart was filled with joy at his presence, but my head knew there were still so many unknowns. Was he a dirty agent? Was he a drug runner? Had his actions gotten my mom killed? For now, however, I could only hold him and give thanks.

Finally, I stood back and held him at arms' length. "Why did you let me believe you were dead, Dad? How could you do that? What happened?" I stammered.

"Kiddo, I can explain everything, I promise." His eyes searched mine for forgiveness, but it wasn't something I was ready to give.

Fritz cautiously stepped in and put his hand on my arm, squeezing it gently. "Listen, I hate to break this up, but we've got to get out of here." I nodded and wiped my tears. After all, I'd found my dad, but we were still in danger. There was no time to catch up and get answers. The longer we stayed in here, the more likely we'd get caught, and then all hell would break loose. "We'll have time for a family reunion later," he said softly. "And we'll make sure you get some answers, okay?" He slapped my dad on the back a little forcefully.

"Okay, you're right." I sniffed and let go of my dad. "Let's get to it."

I struggled to catch my breath and looked around the room for the first time. We were in some kind of huge game room, complete with a pool table, air hockey, darts, foosball, and even a basketball hoop. Screens dotted the walls. A bar area was tucked into a corner, fully stocked. I was surprised Fritz hadn't set up shop and whipped up a batch of margaritas yet. I sure could have used one or three. A lone couch was tucked in the back of the room in a cozy area with two recliners and a coffee table. Of course, my husband had opted to snooze on the pool table instead.

I walked over to poor Michael and rubbed his arm. He opened one eye and, upon seeing me, struggled to sit up.

"He's alive!" Fritz whispered, feigning fear. His face became more serious and he furrowed his brow. "You sober yet, man? You had me a little worried. Good grief, I'd hate to see you on the harder stuff."

Michael looked confused and put his head in his hands. He moaned out loud. "My head is killing me." Looking up at Fritz, his eyes narrowed. "Did you drug me, Fritz?" His face contorted in confusion as he began to stand, and Fritz took a step back.

"Uh," Fritz looked around for help, "let me just mention that your father-in-law tried to *kill* you first. I'm just saying..."

Michael again lowered his head and, upon trying to stand, stumbled to the side. My dad and I both reached out and caught him before he fell over. In doing so, my shirt hiked up and Fritz caught a glimpse of the Ruger tucked into my waistband.

"Why don't I hold that," he said as we struggled to keep Michael standing. He reached over and took the gun, flipping it back and forth casually in his hands. "Thank God we've got a real weapon now."

"Geez, Fritz, be careful with that thing!" I cautioned as I looked back at him. How could anyone be so comfortable with a firearm?

"Emily, come on, I know what I'm doing," he said disdainfully.

Frankly, I was glad to have the gun out of my possession. I'd much rather hold onto my struggling husband than have to deal with that hunk of metal in my pants. How do cops walk around with those things attached to their person for an entire shift? I had been constantly worrying I was going to shoot off part of my ass.

"Why don't you give me that," my dad said. He let go of Michael and gestured toward Fritz with his hand held out.

"Whoa," Darcy said, walking up to him. "For all we know, you're a dirty, drug-running double agent and definitely the reason we're all in this mess. So, thanks, but no. We'll be keeping that, George." She directed a pointed look at Fritz. My dad nodded and dropped his hands in surrender. "You should help out with Michael, anyway."

Fritz suddenly doubled over in pain, nearly dropping the gun. "Damn. Sciatica. Killing me," he squeaked out. Darcy gingerly took the gun from him, leaving Fritz to hobble around the room, grabbing at his leg and wincing. My dad and I steadied Michael, who was still groggy and unable to support his own weight. Fritz finally caught his breath and exhaled in relief.

"Whoo! Man. That hurt." He looked around the room and his gaze stopped on a small baggie. "Uh, you guys mind if I—"

"Don't you even think about it," I growled. Michael tried to step out of our grasp and nearly fell over. Looking up at me, he sighed. "God, babe, I'm so sorry. I'm pathetic. And I feel fuuuunny." Then he let out a small giggle and grinned slightly. I knew it killed him to be helpless like that. But seriously, it was kind of cute.

"Absolutely none of this is your fault," I told him. "If anyone's sorry, it's me." I gave him a kiss on the cheek. His face was rough, the five o'clock shadow now about ten hours old. If possible, he was even more ruggedly handsome than normal, but for the glazed look in his eyes.

"No," my dad interrupted. "If anyone should be sorry, it's me." He paused and looked over to the window, as if weighing options. Taking a deep breath, he continued. "Now that Michael's mobile again, and we're all here, I've come up with a plan." We all stood, attentively listening. "We're going to head out that window." Darcy's jaw dropped. "We're going to have to work fast. Head to the back of the house and shimmy down the drainpipe to the portico. I think we can jump from there." Fritz looked like he'd just swallowed a lemon and rubbed his beard.

"Yeah, well, uh, see, this body doesn't do a lot of shimmying and jumping off of buildings, George..." He patted his big, round belly and jerked his thumb behind him. "I vote secret passage."

My dad walked over to the window and slowly forced it open. Cold air rushed in, and flakes of snow swirled above us. It was pitch dark outside. He expected us to go out in this? Hopefully, he knew where the cars were being held so we could easily get to safety. We'd be dead within an hour out in the elements otherwise. Of course, we might be dead within the hour if we stayed in here too.

"The secret passageway is just where they'll look, don't you get it?" he said firmly. "We have to exit this house, and we have to do it now."

My ears perked up. He was saying "we". Had he changed his mind? Was he going to go with us after all? Could he give up his vendetta against Izzy, if only temporarily, in order to get us to safety? Or was he simply going to lead us all out onto the roof in freezing temps and shut the window behind us, forcing us to leave without him?

Fritz and Darcy walked over and looked out. "I don't know," Fritz said with a frown. "This makes me—"

All of a sudden, Michael interrupted, his head shooting up. "Someone's coming! Quick! Go! Go!" I heard the sound of footsteps echoing from far down the hall, the heavy tread quickly getting louder and louder. Fritz grabbed Darcy, and with amazing agility for a man his size, yanked her over the windowsill out onto the roof. Apparently, the roof escape option wasn't looking so bad to him now. I heard Darcy slip and cry out as she tried to maintain her balance.

"Emily!" Fritz hissed. "Now!" He motioned at me to hurry up. I pulled at Michael while he tried to push me in front of him toward the window.

"Go, Emily. Get out, now!" Michael pleaded. "All of you, go!"

"I'm not leaving you!" I cried. My dad, Fritz, and I pulled at him and he struggled to take a step, yanking us all sideways. His instability was too much for us to cross the distance and get him out the window in the split second that we had.

I shot my gaze up and jerked my head at Fritz. "Go! Just go! Get help!" He shook his head no insistently and instead grabbed my dad, throwing him toward the window.

"You go. I wouldn't last thirty seconds out there!" Fritz had a point. My dad looked back at me frantically and I nodded in agreement. The footsteps were getting closer and closer. We had no time for indecision.

"I'll come back for you, I promise." My dad took one last look at me and jumped out the window. I could hear cursing and slipping as he and Darcy struggled to maintain traction on the icy rooftop.

Fritz slammed the window shut and quickly wiped the snow off the sill.

"Emily, get down. Get down!" he hissed.

I ducked under the pool table and rolled to the center, praying I'd gotten completely out of view. I held my breath and stayed completely still as the door flung open.

• CHAPTER 27 •

"WHAT'S GOING ON IN HERE? It sounds like a herd of elephants walking around." Diego barked. I stared up at the bottom of the pool table, imagining myself invisible. Surely, he felt the coldness of the room. He'd know we had the window open. He'd start looking around and he'd find me! Moving my head just slightly, I saw that I could view him through a small crack by the upper corner of the table's leg. He was still bundled up, as if he'd been outside. Thank God. He might not notice that it was frigid in here. I silently prayed that he couldn't see me. I felt as if I were playing a life-or-death game of hide and seek.

"Sorry, man. Uh, we were just playing a game of pool to pass the time. It's all gooood." Michael sang out. He sounded drunk. "Guess we got a little rowdy." I looked over at the pool cues neatly lined in their holder. *Man,* I thought, *I hope Diego doesn't pay attention to detail.* "This guy here thought he could beat me in a game of golf pool." Michael laughed and stood up shakily, nodding at Fritz. "Wrong! So, now we're going to try some darts, right, old man?" He was trying to stay in between me and Diego so I wouldn't be seen. Plus, I'm pretty sure he was still seeing double and couldn't move much further.

"You wanna play some pool, gringo? Huh? I beat you at pool. I kick your ass at pool," Diego sneered. "Gimme a stick." *Shit.* "Come on, *cabrón,* you think you can play?"

Diego walked up to Michael and, because of the height difference, chest butted him in the belly. I could see the muscles in Michael's back tense up. His fingers spread and began to twitch, as if waiting to attack. I knew Michael could take him out in a heartbeat, but for the semiautomatic weapon in Diego's hands, and the fact that he wasn't quite on top of his game at the present. *Keep calm, babe. Please don't let him provoke you.*

"You think you can—"

Suddenly, a voice called to Diego from down the hall, startling him. He grimaced and stepped back. *"Sí! Un minuto, por favor,"* he shouted loudly over his shoulder. Turning to look back at Michael and Fritz, he hefted his gun and hissed, *"El jefe está aquí."* An evil grin spread across his face. "The fun is just beginning, *mis amigos.*" He turned on his heel and left the room, the door slamming shut behind him.

The room instantly became silent, and I swore I could hear footsteps scurrying on the rooftop outside. Had my dad and Darcy made it to safety? Or would they be caught by *el jefe's* henchmen just outside?

I rolled out from under the pool table and struggled to sit up. Fritz leaned against the far wall, arms crossed, with a shell-shocked look on his face. Michael rested his hands on his knees and took a deep breath before reaching down to help me stand. And my dad's snow-covered face stared at me from outside the window. *Wait, what the?*

I dashed to the window and hefted it open. "Dad, what's going on? You're supposed to be getting help!"

"Darcy's getting help. Don't worry. I helped her down to the back portico and told her where the vehicles are most likely stashed."

"Most likely? It's freezing outside, Dad. What if she can't find them? What if *el jefe* finds her first?"

He struggled a bit as he hefted himself inside the room. His breathing was labored and his skin looked red and ruddy, like a farmer who'd been hard at work doing chores in the snow.

"Darcy's a big girl, Emily. Don't worry." Easy for him to say. He didn't know that Jimmy Choo-wearing woman from Adam. He heaved big gulps of breath as he struggled to catch his own. "She's dressed warm, and she'll figure it out. She's got to. I've got to get the rest of us out of here."

"But she's all alone," I said, wondering about Darcy's survival skills and not feeling too good about them. "What if someone finds her out there? How's she going to handle that? She's got no weapon."

He sighed heavily, rubbing his face with his hand. "Well, actually, she does." He paused and glanced at all of us, a look of chagrin on his face. "Seems we're the ones without a weapon now. Darcy's still got the gun."

• CHAPTER 28 •

OUR ONLY WEAPON WAS NOW BEING TOTED around by a brown-haired Barbie with a bright pink manicure outside in a blizzard at night. I sure hoped my secret agent dad had some badass self-defense skills to get us out of this mess if we got caught escaping. I could've always utilized my own, such as they were. It was Fritz and Michael in his current state that I was most worried about. How on earth would we get my 210-pound husband out the window, across a rooftop, and down a portico when he could barely stand on his own two feet without attracting attention? And with Fritz and his sciatica? This was a recipe for disaster.

The three of us braced Michael and made our way slowly to the window. Fritz kept eyeing the bag of pot sitting out.

"It will give me fortitude," he muttered as he strained to hold up Michael. I could tell he was longing for a hit and hissed at him, "Don't you dare!"

I had to elbow Michael in the ribs and shush him at one point when he started trying to get us all to do the Cotton Eyed Joe. I couldn't wait to get my take-charge, level-headed husband back.

We just reached the window when we again heard footsteps coming from down the hall. We all paused and strained to hear the heavy tread getting closer.

"I'm going out!" my dad commanded. "We've got to hurry! I'll pull his top half while you two get his legs." He hastily threw up the sash and climbed out on the rooftop. Snow again swirled in from above, flakes landing on my lashes. My dad heaved and Fritz and I each grabbed a leg and lifted. Michael attempted to brace himself with his arms to lend a hand. But then suddenly, Fritz dropped Michael's leg and doubled over in pain.

"Dammit!" he hissed. He fell down to one knee, grabbing at his back as the door swung open. Diego hoisted his gun up, aiming the barrel straight at us.

"*¡El Diablo Blanco!*" he whispered in surprise as he saw my dad. A look of reverence crossed his face but was quickly replaced by anger. He looked around, stunned to see both my dad and me there with Fritz and Michael. But if he noticed Darcy was missing, he didn't immediately let on. "*¡Cierra la ventana! ¡Ahora!*" He impatiently motioned my dad inside with the gun.

My dad looked around in a panic. He was already outside, the darkness nearly enveloping him. He could easily just turn and disappear. I silently willed him to do so. But then what would become of us? Did they know the connection between all of us? Had they figured out we weren't just curious passersby that got lost driving around? The thought made my head hurt.

"I knew you bitches wouldn't stay put," Diego said as he looked at me. *God,* I thought, *I hope Darcy is far, far away.* His gaze swung back to my dad. "Don't even think about it, *El Diablo,*" he sneered. *El jefe* will want to see you." With a menacing look in his eyes, he jerked the gun barrel toward me and walked closer. I could smell tequila on him from five feet away, and he had beads of sweat forming on his forehead. "I'll put a bullet right through her head if you take another step." This guy was bloodthirsty and more than a little unbalanced. I didn't doubt him for a minute.

"Oh boy, now Diego's pissed," Michael whispered, his eyes wide and still a bit unfocused. "Get behind me." That was pretty impossible, seeing as he was leaning against the wall. I stayed put with my hands in the air while my dad gingerly crept back inside and shut the window. The frigid air hung in the room and goosebumps prickled on my skin.

Diego began muttering to himself. His finger hovered just above the trigger—a lot closer than I was comfortable with in his current state. He was half drunk, in not much better shape than Michael right now. Had Michael been fully sober and alert, I had no doubt the four of us could have taken charge of the situation and disarmed a drunk Diego. But with Michael and Fritz both compromised and my dad half frozen, that left me, and only me. I didn't like those odds. A wave of nausea swept over me as I stood there, afraid to move. His eyes looked us over wildly. I could see comprehension dawn on his face as he realized Darcy was no longer with us.

"*¡Cabrónes!*" he said, his boots stomping on the floor. "Where's the other girl? The loud one? There were two of you before."

I opened my mouth to speak, unsure of what I was going to say, but my dad cut me off.

"She's long gone by now, Diego. And there's no use trying to find her." Diego's face turned red and splotchy as he realized one of his hostages had escaped. He ran over to the window. "She's a well-trained survivalist, an EMT, and part of the local avalanche search and rescue," my dad continued. Where was he coming up with this? Darcy's only survivalist skills were navigating her suburban neighborhood streets as a teen driver in Ohio. "She's probably halfway down the mountain by now. The cops are going to be swarming this place any minute."

Diego gripped the gun in anger, a vein popping out on his forehead. He stomped over to my dad and hit him across the face with the butt of the gun. I cried out and reached for him, but Michael caught my arm and held me back. An evil grin spread across Diego's face, and his chest heaved with every breath. Blood trickled from my dad's cheek, but his gaze remained level.

"Take me to Izzy," he said, spitting blood. "I'm the one you want. Let these people go. They have nothing to do with this."

Diego's eyes glistened. "Oh, I take you to see Izzy, all right. All in good time, *amigo*. All in good time." Hefting his gun up, he motioned Fritz, Michael, and my dad to go out in the hall. As I began to join them, he stepped in front of me.

"Ah, not you, *amiga*. Not yet. *El jefe* wants to talk to you. Alone.

"Marco!" he yelled down the hall. "*¡Ven aquí!*" After a minute, Marco appeared and the two of them whispered while Diego kept the gun unsteadily trained on my dad. Marco disappeared but came back shortly, he and Diego resuming their animated, hushed discussion.

I could see Michael's eyes beginning to come back into focus as we waited, and he appeared to be standing taller, unassisted. Perhaps his high was finally wearing off. I hoped so, for all of their sakes. He was the best hope they had of escaping. He caught my eye and began mouthing something. I couldn't make out what he was trying to say, but I saw the anguish in his eyes.

Diego, unfortunately, saw his efforts at communication, pushed Marco into the room with me, and slammed the door. I was now alone in the game room with Marco. I could hear Michael arguing with Diego, and then I heard the sound of the gun barrel hitting flesh, followed by a loud grunt. Tears sprang to my eyes. What was he doing to my husband? I rushed to the door, but Marco stopped me. His eyes held a slight look of compassion, and he slowly shook his head. Fear and rage overtook me, and I began to shake. While I wasn't afraid of Marco, Diego was still just beyond the door. If I tried to force my way out of the room now, it would only end badly.

"Sit down," Marco urged, nodding at the couch. "You listen, everything be okay." I could see the doubt in his eyes, and a wave of nausea overtook me. What was going to happen to us? How could I possibly sit in here and wait, as if everything were going to be okay?

Marco reached into his coat pocket and pulled out two small bottles of water. He looked at them briefly, as if considering whether to give me one, and finally handed it to me, avoiding my gaze.

I could hear Diego yelling at the guys to move, and their footsteps quickly retreated down the hall. My mind raced as I thought of ways to overtake Marco. He was old, sure, but that didn't mean he wasn't strong. And he had a gun. I had a...Maglite. Not really a fair match. Not for the first time, I was wishing I still had the Ruger. But could I use it against this old man? He didn't seem like a hardened criminal. He seemed like someone who was resigned to his fate.

I hesitantly looked up at his face. His eyes were downcast, the corners of his mouth turned down in a frown. He looked exhausted. Were middle-of-the-night hostage situations a common thing for him here in the Rockies surrounding Elkston, Colorado? Likely not. He looked like a rancher, not a criminal.

I twisted the lid off my water bottle and gulped it down eagerly. The stress of the evening had made me completely parched. I reached into my pocket and pulled out another protein bar. Chocolate chunk. Normally a flavor I would love. But my stomach protested and I put it away.

Sitting down on the couch, I leaned back and closed my eyes. I wasn't afraid of Marco, and I needed to think. My breathing slowed steadily, and I felt my body quickly begin to relax. Opening my eyes, I noticed Marco staring at me, watching me carefully. Only, after a second, there were two Marcos. Maybe three. Wait. Why was my vision blurry? I tried to say something to him, but speaking felt like a monumental task. Attempting to sit up, I realized I could only move my head, and even then, barely at all. They had drugged me! They'd put something in the water.

Marco put his gun down, slowly walked over, and gently took my wrist, presumably checking my pulse.

"Rest now, *niñita,*" he said as he lifted my legs onto the couch. Very soon he walked out of my line of sight. The last thing I heard was the click of the door as I was helpless to do anything but fall into the depths of sleep.

• CHAPTER 29 •

ANOTHER SMALL CLICK OF THE DOOR HANDLE awoke me and I sat up startled. How long had I been asleep? Minutes? Hours? I wiped a bit of drool from my chin. Man, I was sexy. I blinked my dry eyes, reaching for the water but then remembered the sedative it contained. What had Diego done to the guys? Were they okay? What about Darcy? My pulse raced as I struggled to shake the fog from my brain.

I slowly turned toward the door and was stunned to see Caty from the resort walk in wearing a long, luscious fur coat. She took off her gloves and hat and carefully laid them on a table just inside the door. *Omigod,* I thought. *Why is she here? Does she know Izzy personally?*

"Caty, what are you doing here?" I looked around, panicked. "It's not safe here! How did you get in?"

"I'm sorry?" she said, tilting her head like she didn't understand.

"*¿El jefe está aquí?*" I heard Marco say, walking up to the door. *The boss is here?* Someone grunted, "*Sí.*" He then stuck his head inside and spoke to Caty. "*Grita si me necesitas, Señora.*" *Holler if you need me.*

"Make yourself useful and go find the other girl," she hissed before turning away from him.

Wait a second. What? Caty? I shook my head in confusion. Marco had addressed her as if she were *el jefe*. There's no way Caty was *el jefe*. Wasn't Izzy *el jefe?* But where was Izzy? What the heck was going on?

"Oh, poor Emily. You look confused," she said, drawing out the last word as she stroked her fur coat. "What can I clear up for you?" Her round brown eyes stared at me imploringly. "Hmmm?"

I didn't respond. I couldn't stop staring at her and trying to sort out everything in my head.

"Jorge—oops, sorry, *your dad*—is just fine, by the way. Well, for now." She lifted one eyebrow and a grin played at her lips. "And those other two?" She laughed. "Tank and Diego are taking care of them." *Tank? Who's Tank? Her giant boyfriend?* "They won't cause any trouble until it's time to dispose of their bodies. I mean really, Emily, they're both quite *large*, don't you think? Though I bet that husband of yours is a lot fun in the sack," she said thoughtfully, tapping her chin.

My nostrils flared but I managed to keep my temper in check. What the hell was going on? I was shocked that Caty was apparently one of the bad guys. Bad enough to be called *el jefe*. She must be someone very close to Izzy, who could be anywhere at this moment.

I silently reminded myself that Caty's use of the present tense when referring to Michael and Fritz was a good thing. And I resolved to not fall prey to her sexual remarks about Michael. She was right, after all.

"I've been following you for a while, Emily." She took off her coat and laid it carefully over the sofa. Her eyes sparkled. "Did you ever wonder just how you were so fortunate as to win your honeymoon trip?" I slowly stood up, turned to her, and kept silent. She walked closer to me. "Why, you were the only one to receive an entry form." She laughed at her cleverness.

Caty was behind our honeymoon getaway? I thought a local travel agency in California had put on that contest? No wonder the winning notification was so quick. It was no contest at all. Ugh. I should have known it was too good to be true. Silently, I cursed myself for filling it out in the first place. We should have just stayed at the B&B in La Jolla.

"Oh, I would have gotten you here one way or another," she said, as if reading my mind. "You see, just a few months ago, I got wind that your dad might not actually be dead. *Cabrón*, he should have been taken by the gators, just like your mom."

My hand involuntarily shot up to strike her, and she grabbed my arm. "I wouldn't do that if I were you." Her eyes flickered toward the door. "I've got a loyal staff armed with semiautomatics, and they might be tempted to use them on you and your sweet dad sooner than later."

We locked eyes and I weighed my options, my chest heaving with anger. I knew there was no way I'd get out of this place alive on my own with armed guards lurking around the house. I stopped resisting, and she let go of my arm. I dropped my hand and bit my lip. The physical pain distracted me long enough to calm my urge to smack her...for now. How dare she speak of my mom's death like that.

She walked to the couch, motioning me to join her. I stood where I was, arms crossed.

"Suit yourself. Anyway, as I was saying, I found out your dad was alive, but I was unable to get an idea of his exact location. He kept moving from one place to another." She sat down, stretched her legs out on the couch, and sighed. "It's so very annoying to have to tie up loose ends. But I knew if he was really alive, he'd try to come to your rescue if he thought you were in danger."

I'm not so sure he would have. I had been in danger before in the past year, and he hadn't so much as shown his face.

Caty continued. "So I had to get you here. I figured I'd let you and your hubs enjoy a few days of wedded bliss, then suddenly, you both inexplicably, disappear." Her eyes brightened as if she were describing a fairytale. "News of your shocking disappearance would make it back to your secret agent dad somehow, and he'd come running." She took a piece of candy out of a dish on the coffee table and popped it into her mouth. "Problem solved! Right?"

How ironic that my dad had blown up a building to get Izzy's attention, and at the same time, one of Izzy's henchmen—er, henchwomen—had been going to great lengths to get his.

"I see you're still confused." She tilted her head to one side. "That's okay. I've got time.

"Mmmm, you really should try this chocolate." She lifted the dish toward me and I shook my head. "No? You sure? Okay then."

I wanted to take the dish and shove it down her throat. If only I still had the Ruger on me. I'd get myself out of this place one way or another. My mind raced. Where was Darcy? Was she safe? Had she found a way to get out of here? She was our only hope, and the thought wasn't very comforting.

Caty had continued talking, and I forced myself to focus on what she was saying.

"...so I knew your dad would be none the wiser. I'd put Fernando in charge of the search party. After all, you and your beefcake husband would go missing on one of our trails at the resort. Probably fall off the side of the mountain in the end." She rolled her eyes like all of this was so very trivial. "Details, details," she said. I glared at her.

"I don't like to come to the US often," she turned and looked at me. "It's quite dangerous for someone of my...position. But I had to get him here and personally finish the job." She laughed. "But little did I know you'd take care of the logistics for me." A devious smile formed on her face. "We didn't have to do a thing. You all came straight here."

"Just explain something to me first," I said, staring her in the eye. "I don't understand. Why did Izzy hire *you* to kill my dad? Why couldn't he just do it himself?" The thought of tiny little Caty—who I had thought was just a front desk person at a luxury resort—being a hired assassin was ludicrous. Her scary looking boyfriend, maybe, but not her.

"Oh, Emily." She shook her head, stood up and took my hands. "Catriona Isaguirre at your service." She gave me a wicked smile and then looked at me with disdain. "Don't you get it? I'm the new Izzy."

• CHAPTER 30 •

"WERE YOU ASSUMING IZZY WAS A MAN?" She laughed as she let go of my hands. "I'm disappointed in you, Emily. You, of all people, should know that a woman can be just as powerful as a man." Her brown eyes flashed. "You've been abandoned, lost everything, and come back to make something of yourself. I do read the papers, you know. Especially when it concerns the daughter of someone on my payroll. Or, rather, formerly on my payroll."

She turned to walk away and I wiped my hands on my pants. I couldn't stand to have one speck of her on me. How was Caty actually Izzy? Caty, who couldn't even be thirty years old, was head of a Mexican drug cartel?

She whipped back around. "You see, your dad used to be a good, old FBI agent. You knew that, right?" She stared at me, and I forced my face to remain neutral. "Or did he hide that from you?" Her eyebrows shot up and she whispered, "You didn't know all along? Well, tsk, tsk, tsk. At least it wasn't only us that he lied to.

"Anyway, he was honest as the day is long, I was told. An upstanding federal agent. And he kept tabs on our family's business back in the day...before we turned him." She looked up at me to gauge my reaction. I remained completely still, practicing deep breathing, inhaling through the nose, exhaling out the mouth. In my head, I visualized punching her in the nose.

She continued. "We always managed to play nice when Jorge was around. We doctored communications and drops to his advantage to make him feel useful, like he was doing a good job keeping us under control." She sighed and smiled. "Stupid feds. They think we don't know what's going on, but," she said, tapping her temple, "we're smarter than that. We've got people on the inside."

I took a deep breath and wondered just how long she'd stay in here with me. Maybe Darcy and the police were already on their way back up the mountain. I had to stall her to keep all of us alive.

"Who, pray tell," I said, "was that? Who's your person on the inside?" I didn't actually know any FBI agents—well, other than my dad—so any name she gave me would be irrelevant. I was just trying to draw out the conversation.

She fanned her hand across her face. "Oh, no one you'd know. The ex-wife of a now-retired agent. She was good at intercepting encrypted emails and such. We compensated her nicely.

"Anyway," she continued, "somewhere along the line, my uncle forged a relationship with your dad. Good old Uncle Izzy, God rest his soul." She made a sign of the cross—hypocrite—and kept on. "Uncle Iz agreed we'd play nice with the locals, and in exchange, your dad would occasionally look the other way when we had altercations with rival cartels." She sighed as if relishing a sweet memory, but then her face turned ugly. "However, I know this is a tactic they all use to get us to wipe each other out and do their dirty work for them. *Cabrónes.*" Then she let loose a string of Spanish words even I couldn't understand. Her face turned red and I took a small step back.

Suddenly, she stopped and held up her hands in a classic meditation pose, thumb making a circle with her index finger. Her demeanor changed and she slowly relaxed. "And then, Uncle Izzy got your dad to come to our side. To act as a double agent."

In my head, I was going through the unredacted parts of the FBI file, all of which were in keeping with her story, so far. I was hoping she'd keep talking so I'd learn everything that had been blacked out in Fritz's documents. Everything the FBI was still trying to keep a secret.

"Your dad even traveled to some of our suppliers in Colombia and Honduras. In a few short years, he learned the network. It was amazing all the information he could retain." She spoke reverently of him, her words coming faster and faster. "He earned everyone's respect. He would leak information to us about raids, get drugs easily passed over the border into the US. He was known as *'El Diablo Blanco,' The White Devil.* I was in awe of him. He was untouchable, a valued asset to us. A member of the family."

It was painful to hear someone like her speak of my dad like that. Reading about his nefarious activities while supposedly an upstanding federal agent was one thing, but having them relived by a person who had witnessed them was another.

"Then why try to have him killed?" I asked incredulously. "You turned him into a double agent. It sounds like he became pretty indispensable to you."

"Your dad pulled the wool over our eyes. He became a *traidor,*" she hissed at my interruption. Huh. Funny that *she* would call him a traitor. He was betraying his own country, not hers.

"How did he betray *you,* exactly? You had a corrupt FBI agent on your bankroll."

"Ah, *Emilycita,* that is only what we thought." Her head shot up, the anger returning to her eyes. "It turns out he was playing us all along."

A loud commotion from the hallway interrupted us. The door handle clicked, and I swung around. Diego backed in, dragging my bruised and bloodied dad with him. His hands were bound behind his back. One eye was nearly swollen shut, his lip was cut and bleeding, and he was bent at the waist as if pained him too much to stand up straight. What had Diego done to him? Fury engulfed me.

Then I saw Diego's face. He didn't look much better than my dad. His eye was beginning to swell and his cheek was bruised and cut. I smiled inside at the thought of someone getting at least one good swing at him.

"Diego!" Caty said sharply. "What have you done?" She walked around me and looked at my dad, holding his head high, pain evident on his face. "You were to save him for me!"

She cupped my dad's face in her hands. Her voice was low and soothing as she said, "Oh, my dear, dear friend." She forced his gaze to meet hers. "Your hell is only just beginning." Then she pushed his face roughly to the side. He winced in pain.

It crushed me to see my dad like this. I tried to go to him, only to be stopped by Caty as she wrenched my arm.

"Get back here, you little brat," she growled. I fought her until Diego hoisted his gun and pointed it at my father's torso. I immediately stilled.

Diego lowered the weapon and addressed Caty. *"Lo siento, señora."* Jerking his head toward my dad, he continued. "Those three *amigos,"* he spat out, "they tried to all attack me at once." He rubbed his jaw carefully. "That big one, he is strong." He shrugged his shoulders. "But then Tank showed up and took care of things." Caty nodded, knowingly. I shuddered to think of what he'd done to Michael and Fritz. Diego continued. "Still no sign of the girl. I'm sure the elements have gotten to her by now. She's useless to them."

"Everything's going to be okay, honey," my dad whispered to me. He smiled a half smile, his cut lip oozing more blood.

"*¡Cállate!*" Caty exclaimed, raising her hand to hit him. But her hand halted in midair. My dad flinched, waiting for the blow that never came.

"I still need some more information from you, *mi amor*." Caty lowered her hand. She closed her eyes and exhaled slowly.

"Diego. Get some towels. He's bleeding all over my floor," she snapped.

Diego nodded, threw my dad roughly to the ground, and stepped out into the hall. My dad landed on his side and struggled to sit up. Caty withdrew a very small handgun, waving it in his face.

"Don't get any ideas, Jorge."

My dad smiled a wry grin and leaned back against the wall. He closed his eyes and sighed.

"What information could you possibly need from me anymore, Caty. I'm not in the game. I know nothing." He coughed, wincing in pain. "Your family killed my wife and tried to kill me." He spat blood on the floor. Caty's eyes darted to the small red pool. "Why would I help you now?"

"I'm sure I can give you reason to." She turned the gun toward me and released the safety. "You betrayed us," she hissed at him.

"We treated you like *la familia*. Uncle Izzy loved you." Though she spoke to him, her eyes bore down on me, the gun in her hand never wavering.

"Izzy wanted out, Caty. He wanted to clear his family's name. He came to me—"

"No! You are lying!" She shot the gun, the bullet missing my shoulder by a fraction of an inch.

I screamed and jumped back. My heart hammered out of control. That bitch just tried to shoot me!

"Caty, what are you doing?" my dad yelled. Somehow, he had pushed himself to a standing position. With a look of pure determination in his eyes, he lowered his shoulder and barreled toward her.

She turned to aim at him, and I ran in, forcing her hands toward the ceiling just as he reached her. The gun went off a second time, shattering a light bulb. Shards of glass rained down on us as we all tumbled to the ground. The gun flew out of reach and I wrestled with Caty to keep her from crawling after it. My dad used his weight to keep her down. With his hands tied behind his back, it was his only defense.

"Get the gun, Emily!" he shouted. He reached out for it with his foot.

"Diego! Tank!" Caty screamed. Her fingernails scratched at my face as I tried to muffle her screams. I heard loud footsteps pounding down the hallway, and soon the door was thrown open.

"*¡Señora!*" Diego yelled, out of breath, when he saw Caty on the floor. He raised his gun to the ceiling and shot off a round of ammo. The rat-a-tat-tat of the semiautomatic's bullets pounded in my ears. We all instinctively stopped moving.

"Get off her!" Diego commanded. His face was a combination of excitement and fury, as if this kind of violence thrilled him.

My chest heaved, and I slowly climbed off, releasing Caty's arms. Sweat rolled into my eyes from the exertion of the brief encounter. My dad rolled onto his side, his eyes still pinned on hers.

"*Vete a la mierda,*" Caty cursed at me as she struggled to breathe. *Go to hell.* Diego ran to her, helping her sit upright. She had been cut in the fall, and blood trickled down her cheek. Diego reached toward her face, but she swatted him away.

"*Cabrón,*" she again directed at my dad. She spat at him, narrowly missing his face. "This family gave you so much."

Caty stood up and walked over to where her gun was lying on the floor. By my calculations, based on credible cinematic examples such as the movie "Clue", I guessed there were maybe three bullets left. Or five? Could different handguns hold varying amounts of bullets? Who the hell knew?

"And you betrayed us," Caty continued.

My mind continued to race. Diego probably had three hundred bullets in his magazine. I really had no idea. So Caty's bullets were inconsequential. The odds were not looking good. And dammit, I had to pee! I tried to put that out of my mind and focus on the life and death situation instead.

Not wanting to draw attention to myself, I remained quiet. But Caty picked up the gun and pointed it at me. So much for becoming invisible.

"Next time I won't miss." She gave my dad a wicked smile and waited a beat, wiping the sweat from her brow and in the process, smearing the blood on her cheek. Her normally straight, sleek and beautiful hair was a mess. The put-together woman now looked like the crazed lunatic she really was.

"You turned on us," she spat out. "You betrayed us. You'd never come over to our side after all. Uncle Izzy was a kind soul, and you used him to learn all about the business so you could ruin us. So you could—what, win some kind of award? 'Special Agent of the Year?'"

My dad scoffed at her. "More like so I could do my job. So I could take down a multibillion-dollar cartel and play just a little part in the war against drugs."

"Emily," my dad looked at me, begging me with his eyes to believe him. "I was never a double agent. I became part of a special task force with the DEA and the Mexican police. After years of getting nowhere with the Morales cartel, we decided on a new approach." He looked at Caty and glared. "An approach that would sacrifice my good name."

Caty cursed and backhanded my dad, hurting her own hand in the process. He didn't miss a beat and kept talking.

"It was decided that I'd play the role of a fallen agent. That I'd come to their side so I could learn everything about them in hopes of turning someone at the top. But we knew we had a mole at the agency, so only a handful of people knew the full story. We had to keep everything under a cone of silence for the mission to be successful."

Was that why some of the file was still redacted? Because of the mole, and the fact that not everyone at the FBI was privy to what was really going on?

"I was able to turn the elder Izzy. The Morales family is his mother's, and he said it was time to get out."

"You shamed my grandmother and her legacy!" Caty spat, shaking her bruised hand.

"Izzy said he wanted to bring peace to the family!" my dad yelled.

"Ha! Peace? Instead, he brought about his own death!"

"You!" my dad hissed. "You *killed* Izzy?"

"For the last time," Caty screamed, "*I am Izzy*!" Her voice echoed in the room, followed by deafening silence. Caty's face was filled with righteous fury. The gun shook in her hands, still aimed at my chest.

My dad dropped his head. His shoulders sagged in defeat.

"*You* tried to have us killed, it wasn't him after all." He sighed heavily. "I knew in my heart it wasn't him." He paused and looked at Caty. The silence was deafening. "You'll never be the leader Izzy was."

And then I heard it. The unmistakable click of the hammer being cocked. I immediately reacted to what I knew was inevitable. Jumping back, I looked down at my chest and waited for the burst of pain. But no shot ever came. My head shot up to see Caty shaking the gun, slamming it against the wall. *Click.* Again, nothing.

"*¿Señora?*" Diego questioned, his trigger finger at the ready on the semiautomatic.

Caty's arm shot up and she grabbed his gun, aiming it at my dad.

"No!" I screamed, launching myself at her. The gun fired. Bullets sprayed around the room, obliterating everything in their path.

From the opposite side of the room, I heard the unmistakable sound of shattering glass and swung my head around as I landed on top of Caty. I couldn't believe what I was seeing. As my breath caught in my throat, two figures dressed all in black came crashing through the windows, Special Ops style.

• CHAPTER 31 •

"DEA! NOBODY MOVE! Hands where I can see them!" the bigger one roared in a deep voice. The two landed heavily just inside the room, dressed in combat gear complete with guns, ammo, night vision goggles, body armor, and helmets. Diego attempted to lift his gun from underneath Caty, only to get shot in the arm. He cursed and dropped the weapon.

"I'm a federal agent!" my dad yelled out. "Don't shoot!"

"Then don't move," the smaller one ordered. A female, from the sound of it. In all of their gear, it was impossible to tell who was what.

The two unhooked themselves from their rappelling gear and walked farther into the room, guns drawn. The bigger one secured the semiautomatic, frisked Diego, and roughly placed him in handcuffs.

"She's got a handgun too," I said, nodding my head at Caty, my voice shaking. I kept my hands in the air as ordered. Relief flooded through me as I realized we might finally be safe.

"Bitch," Caty muttered under her breath.

The smaller DEA agent squatted down, jabbed a knee into Caty's back, frisked her, and secured the handgun.

"Catriona Isaguirre," she said, "you are under arrest for the murder of Elizabeth Potens, a litany of drug trafficking charges which I'll let the US Attorney explain later, attempted murder, and false imprisonment. Oh, and the Mexican government wants to speak to you too." She looked at her partner as she swung Caty around to face her. "Am I missing anything?" The agent's voice sounded a bit familiar, but I couldn't place it. It almost had a Boston twang to it. Had I met her before? Doubtful. Most likely the adrenaline coursing through my veins was making me hear things differently.

"George Potens?" she said, turning to my dad.

"Yes?"

The woman removed her night vision goggles and slowly began to take her helmet off, revealing sleek blonde hair tied in a low bun. Her back was to me, and she turned my dad around to untie his hands.

"Do I know you?" my dad asked.

"Nope," she said, "but I know all about you. And her." The agent tipped her head toward me.

She turned around where I could see her face, and my eyes grew wide. I couldn't believe what I was seeing. Savannah! Big-haired, big-boobed Savannah was a Special Ops DEA agent? Gone was the makeup. Gone was the big hair. Gone was the Texas accent!

I struggled to find words. My head swung over to her partner as he removed his goggles and helmet. Dirk walked purposefully toward me, dragging Diego with him before depositing him on the floor with Caty.

"How ya doing, Emily?" he asked with a wink. I stared at him with my mouth hanging open.

"Big G," he said, grabbing my dad in a hug.

Big G? Those two knew each other?

"Oh, Dirk, you are a sight for sore eyes," my dad said. They patted each other twice on the back in typical man-hug fashion. My dad looked up at Dirk and furrowed his brow.

"You were following Emily, weren't you? You were at the wedding."

Dirk shrugged. "I may have been in attendance, inconspicuously, hovering somewhere in the background, hoping you'd show your face." He lowered his head. "She was beautiful, by the way," he whispered.

My dad nodded, a look of regret in his eyes.

Dirk had been the one at the wedding? Was he the one who gave Father the note? Why?

So many questions ran through my head. How did they know we were here? How did they know the exact room we were in? And where were Michael, Fritz, and Darcy? After all, Marco was still somewhere out there with a gun, as well as Tank. No telling who else Caty had brought up with her. I shook myself out of my stupor and found my voice.

"I hate to break up this reunion," I said forcefully, "but we have to find everyone else. Michael, Fritz, and Darcy are still in danger."

"Roger that," Dirk said as he and Savannah tied Diego and Caty together, back to back on the floor. "You wanna stay with these two?" he asked Savannah. "I'll scout out the rest of the house?"

"I'm coming with you!" I insisted. I couldn't sit around anymore, unsure whether my husband was still alive. I was jumping out of my skin.

I ran to the door and flung it open, just as Dirk yelled at me to wait. Turning down the hall, I ran smack into a solid belly. Dammit! Tank! I recoiled and tried to yank myself out of his grasp, but he refused to let go.

"Emily. Emily!"

I looked up and the air rushed out of my lungs. The face that looked down at me was Michael's, not Tank's. Darcy immediately followed, with Fritz slowly bringing up the rear. Relief coursed through my body as I collapsed into his arms.

• CHAPTER 32 •

THE SUN WAS RISING, creating an almost blinding scene up on the mountaintop that morning. The orange rays shone brightly and the snowy landscape sparkled. The beauty was in contrast to the remainder of the scene—police cruisers parked willy nilly, lights flashing, walkie talkies screeching, a dozen law enforcement officers walking to and from the house.

Agencies of all sorts flooded the property. DEA, FBI, the local PD. Caty, Tank, and Diego were taken into custody immediately. Marco, upon encountering an angry Darcy in the barn with the Ruger, had already fled the scene.

We were interrogated for hours. My dad was separated from the rest of us. The FBI was eager to get their hands on him, wanting to know just what he'd been doing for the last eighteen months. They weren't the only ones. Dirk did make sure to stay by his side as much as he could.

While the current and former federal agents were all being questioned and debriefed, Darcy, Fritz, Michael and I filled each other in on what had gone one while we were separated. We sat in the sun-filled chef's kitchen, each of us nursing a large cup of coffee while Fritz rooted around in the fridge and cupboards for food. Coming up with eggs, sausage, peppers, and potatoes, he set about making us a delicious hash. Of course, I was so hungry, anything would have sounded delicious at that point.

I wolfed down my plate and went to get more, beating both Fritz and Michael to seconds. Darcy, of course, only had one plate full. Now that my belly was leaning toward full and I was no longer hangry, I started peppering Darcy with questions. It turns out she had escaped the room unscathed and headed for the barn, where she found the SUV. Opting for quiet over speed, she chose the bandito method and took off on a horse instead. Upon reaching the abandoned mining road, she was nearly run over by Dirk and Savannah, who had apparently placed a tracking device on my phone and a listening device in my purse.

They had followed Michael and me from California after breaking into our house and figuring out our honeymoon location. Dirk was certain I knew my dad was still alive and had tried to bait me with the note at the wedding, hoping I'd make contact. At the resort, they'd commandeered a room from a guest, paying him handsomely for his silence, so that they could keep an eye on my every move. It turned out Dirk had taken my phone the night I thought I had lost it and placed the tracking device on it. They'd followed us up that trail the next day, thinking I had set up a secret meeting with my dad. Since that didn't happen, Savannah had then dropped a listening device into my purse when chatting with me the following morning at the spa.

On one hand, I was irritated that I'd been so easily compromised. Bugged and tracked without a clue? On my honeymoon, no less? *My God, what had they heard?!* On the other hand, I was thankful. Their tracking had saved our lives. But still, it was difficult for me to look either of them in the eye. No wonder Dirk kept winking at me.

When Darcy had run into them on the road, they knew there was trouble, her being out on horseback in the middle of a snowstorm and all. The two of them identified themselves as federal agents, which relieved her to no end. She told them what was going on and where we were. They told her to head back to the barn and stay there. She did go to the barn, but only to return the horse, with no intention of staying. Before she could head to the house, she was surprised by Marco, who had been sent out to find her. She pulled the Ruger on him and told him she knew how to use it. Startled but apparently not too upset, he didn't put up a fight and instead took Caty's Hummer and drove off the property.

"He kept saying, *'Chingate, cabrón.'* I really think he was thanking me," Darcy insisted. I didn't have the heart to tell her otherwise.

After Marco drove off, Darcy made her way back to the house and, through a window, witnessed Fritz and Michael being held by Tank. They'd been tied to chairs, back to back, arms wrapped behind them. Tank had apparently partaken of the same tequila as Diego and had fallen asleep, lucky for them. Darcy snuck in and quietly untied the guys, but not before he awakened. Michael dove for his knees, taking him down, and Fritz sat on him, rendering him immobile.

"I've got skills," Fritz said, rubbing his beard as she described the scene. "I do have skills."

They then used Darcy's scarf to tie him up and gagged him with Fritz's sock.

"Knocked him right out again," he laughed with glee.

Upon hearing the commotion and gunfire upstairs, they left him there and ran up, whereupon they ran smack into me.

"I'm so glad you're okay, babe," Michael kept saying, holding my hand. "I heard the gunfire and I thought Dirk and Savannah were too late." He rubbed his face up and down, his eyes red from exhaustion. "It was like déjà vu," he said, referring to a very similar incident last year. "Can we please never do that again?" I laughed and leaned forward, my forehead touching his.

"You got it, babe," I whispered before planting a kiss firmly on his lips. "I promise."

My dad was temporarily released from questioning several hours later but was going to be kept in FBI custody until everything could be sorted out. His old friend Tony's ex-wife had been the mole all along, the one that compromised the mission from the beginning. Tony was the friend he was supposed to be meeting when he and my mom disappeared in the swamps of Louisiana. Now that the mole had safely been identified and dealt with, my dad's trust in the FBI was reestablished. I still wasn't feeling any warm fuzzies toward them, however.

Finally able to get some time with my dad without being under the threat of imminent death, he and I separated ourselves from the group so we could talk in private. I made sure that other people were still in sight, however, as I was half afraid he would take off, never to be seen again. Talk about trust issues.

We sat in the living room of the mansion, a huge room with comfortable, overstuffed, gray leather couches, a separate reading nook, and a smartly camouflaged television. We sat on opposite ends of the couch, and my dad began to tell me the story of the accident, how he and my mom had been run off the road by a large black Hummer. How he had to leave my mom's body to climb to safety but eventually passed out. How, days later, he awoke on the swamp boat of a bayou family. He'd suffered a concussion, several broken ribs, and other internal injuries that led to severe infection. The family had come across him while trolling for gators, rescued him from the swamp, and nursed him back to health for six months. Luckily, he didn't have any identification on him that linked him to the FBI, or they likely would have killed him on the spot. Swamp people don't tend to like "Big Brother."

Once he was healed enough to venture back to civilization, and, knowing there was a price on his head, he carefully reached out to some contacts he thought he could trust. Unfortunately, one of those contacts was Tony, whose ex-wife was still up to her old tricks, and informed Caty that he was still alive. Wisely not willing to stay in one place for any length of time, my dad flitted around the country, occasionally stopping in Texas to watch over me, and at other times, bouncing from one C-IZZY property to another, trying to track down the elder Izzy, not knowing he was already dead. One year later, he landed here.

I was still having a hard time reconciling what I'd heard. A week ago, I'd thought my dad—the completely innocuous, real estate entrepreneur—was dead. And now...this. How was this all going to work itself out? Would I even be able to see my now-alive dad? Or would he be locked up for falsifying his death and defecting from the FBI? Would he be punished or hailed a hero?

I looked over at Michael, who still sat in the kitchen shoveling food down his throat. From the look of things, I guessed he still had the munchies. Darcy sat across from him, head on the table, resting atop her folded arms. Her eyes were closed and I couldn't tell whether or not she was truly asleep. Fritz had found the liquor cabinet and was enjoying three fingers of what I'm sure was top-of-the-line whiskey, as he leaned precariously back on the kitchen chair, threatening to topple over. After having been through so much together, where would we go from here?

• CHAPTER 33 •

Three months later

DARCY HAD GOTTEN HER BREAKOUT STORY, which aired the very next morning and sent the ratings at KVKX through the roof. After receiving multiple offers from larger markets (sadly, none from CNN), she declined them all and instead chose to move to Dallas and work for Fritz as an investigative assistant. She said she may go for her PI license eventually, but wanted to spend some time enjoying working at a job that allowed her to eat whatever she wanted and not have weekly appointments with the dermatology and aesthetic center. She even convinced Fritz to rent out some private space for their offices so she wouldn't have to listen to his "prehistoric music." Fritz's wife, Zoey, was very appreciative of this move, and eventually came back home.

Fritz had grumbled that it was like having two wives now, but I noticed he said it with a slight grin. I don't think he minded too much. The last I heard, things were working out well, though Fritz was trying to convince Darcy and Zoey that they should all relocate to Colorado for the sake of his sciatica. Darcy told him to shut up, get off his ass, and go to physical therapy.

My dad was cleared of all federal criminal charges and relieved of his duties with the FBI after a thorough investigation and psychiatric analysis. The City of Elkston wasn't so understanding, however, and charged him with destruction of property for the explosion, which had damaged nearby infrastructure. He pled no contest and was sentenced to community service. He now lives in a tiny cabin along the banks of the Big Thompson, which suits him just fine. I wish he were in California with us, but just knowing he was still alive and free to do as he pleases makes my heart happy.

Caty is currently awaiting trial for her crimes, which are too numerous to list. The Morales cartel was severely impacted first by Izzy's murder, then by Caty's arrest. The work my dad and Izzy had already begun to break up the cartel had been somewhat successful, but my dad still worried that rival cartels would just take up the slack. The war against drugs is never-ending.

I'm happy to say that Maria and Candy enjoyed their time in the Golden State so much that they decided to take up residence after we returned. Candy started working for me at the shop, while working towards her teaching certificate, and Maria has become a personal trainer at a local gym. They decided to become roommates and have a tiny apartment about ten minutes from us and only a couple of blocks from the beach.

Michael and I came back to California as soon as things were mostly settled regarding my dad. I am happily back at my little antique shop and doing what I can to rehab our new home. Michael, while busy juggling several construction projects, has put the renovation of our house into high gear, measuring, knocking down walls, and playing the part of the overprotective father-to-be. We'll welcome a new bundle of joy just in time for summer. Fritz has already given himself the role of godfather. Heaven help us.

Life is good. Who knows where our next adventure will take us...

ABOUT THE AUTHOR

Maggie Aldrich is an avid reader, indie author, and yoga instructor who tends to catastrophize all situations.

"Good grief, you should become a writer, you're always making stuff up!" her family said. And so she did.

Maggie lives on an acreage in middle America with her husband, daughter, cats, and other various unattended wild animals.

PLEASE LEAVE A REVIEW! Reviews are the lifeblood of authors.

Join the Book Junkies and never miss an update or new release!
http://maggiealdrichwrites.com/thebookjunkies/

Website: www.maggiealdrichwrites.com
Email: maggie@maggiealdrichwrites.com
Facebook: www.facebook.com/maggiealdrichwrites
Twitter: @AldrichWrites

Made in the USA
Coppell, TX
16 April 2020

20266440R00174